THE

DETECTIVE

AND THE

CRIMINAL

A BLACK LOVE DETECTIVE STORY BOOK 5

ANTWAN FLOYD SR.

CRIME FICTION MEDIA

CONTENTS

A CRIME FICTION MEDIA RELEASE

Dedicated to

My loyal supporters and faithful readers

Monique Hagger & Yasmeen Muhammed

Also By

BLACK LOVE DETECTIVE NOVELS
Piece Keeper
Cannibal in the City
Body Bags & Last Rites
A Pound of Flesh, An Ounce of Blood

Paperbacks:
Crew Love
Crew Love pt. 2 "The Black Mob"
Dope Fiction "Alpha Female"
Dope Fiction pt. 2 "Sigma Female"
Danielle Lovelace Vigilante for Hire
Purple Reign "A Trigger Brown Mystery"
The Addiction "An Anthology"

Ebooks:
Wild 100's
Sperm Donor
The Last Transmission of a Gangster
12 Months of Murder: Introduction to Seduction
12 Months of Murder: Reasonable Doubt
12 Months of Murder: The Life and Times of Jade Leskiv Vol. 1

CHAPTER ONE

In an abandoned house in Englewood at 5. am. Three gunshots rang out from a Glock- two to the heart, one to the head execution-style; he slumped over.

"I thought you were laying low?" Noble said as he scrolled through his phone.

"I am."

"A dead man at your feet is laying low. I thought we came here for a specific reason?"

"We did."

"Dropping bodies wasn't the reason."

"The reasons were modified."

He shook his no. "No more modifications."

"Don't worry, taking him out was a long overdue debt. I'm not forgetting the bottom line."

"As long as you don't forget." She didn't respond; he continued. "How many years it's been since you been gone?"

"Too many to mention, not long enough for folks with a chip on their shoulder the size of the Sears Tower to forget."

"The Willis Tower."

"What?"

"It ain't been the Sears Tower for years."

"Fuck all that; it's always the Sears Tower in my eyes."

"Where are you going?"

"Outsource some work, head back to Detroit. I won't be here long."

"Pepper Red, back to Detroit? What you have me come with you for if you were going to boot me out of the city? I'm not leaving you here alone. You know I have a network out here."

"You worry too much; I'll be fine. I'll have a better shot at staying under the radar the fewer people know I'm back home. I'll reach out if I need to.

***

CHAPTER TWO

For better or worse, he was here now, started with a partner now he was riding solo for a bit of a while anyway until Parker came home. It had been three months since being violated back to Joliet to serve the remainder of his time, he had spent most of that time in Cook County, and the fact that he made it back to Joliet as soon as he had was a miracle most spent a year or more waiting to transfer to their new home. Black had yet to take on another case but promised himself whatever he earned, and he would still split the profit with Parker.

He went to the office every day, waiting for a call. Now and then, someone stopped in, but either the case didn't interest him, they couldn't afford the rates, or they were just curious about the business being on the block. People in the neighborhood were getting used to seeing him there. They often asked for Parker; at one point, he was there much more than Black. He had a deal with the lady across the street, Ms. Jones; he would join her for a game of Tonk once a week, and she would keep an eye out for his business and call him if anything suspicious happened. He figured it was her way of feeling useful, and she could probably use the company, so he conceded after a bit of arguing.

He sat in the waiting area reading *"Nigger: The Strange Career of a Troublesome Word"* by Randall Kennedy. The doorbell rang, and Black stood facing the door after walking over and opening the door. Staring back was a teenage boy about the same height as him, with red hair, freckles, scruffy beard. He had the bluest eyes staring back at Black.

"Can I help you?" Black asked, staring at the young boy; seeing a white kid in this neighborhood was strange.

"Looking for work."

Black laughed. "Yeah, what kind of work do you do?"

"Whatever you need."

Black looked around the boy to see if he was alone or not. "What are you doing around here? Where are your people at?"

"I'll do whatever you need. Just trying to do the right thing and make a few bucks."

Black reached into his pocket and pulled out five twenty-dollar bills. He handed them to the boy. "Here."

The boy took it and looked at it strangely. "What's this for?"

"Nothing, I have nothing for you to do here, but you can have the money."

The boy attempts to give the money back. "I have to earn it; my uncle Mickey says ain't nothing in life free- sooner or later someone will come to collect a debt, and I may not like the interests."

Black laughed. "Your uncle Mickey sounds like a smart man."

"He has his moments. So, what work do you have for me?"

"Look, kid, my word as a man; you don't owe me anything."

The kid stuffed the money into his pocket, nodded at Black then turned to leave. Black closed the door and went back to reading his book. Ten minutes later, the bell rang again, and the door opened. He thought it may have been Trigger, his on-again-off-again "friends" with benefits, or Pops, his father. He stood to go and meet the unannounced guest. He froze in his tracks when he spotted the person. "Pepper Red."

She smiled. "That's how you address your mama now?"

Black stared, mouth open.

"You hate me so much I can't get a hug?"

Black slowly walked toward his mother and wrapped his arms around her. He hugged her as tight as he could. "What are you doing here, ma?"

"Long story, but I missed you."

Black stepped back and took in everything that was his mother. She hadn't changed much. Pepper Red was taller than he was at average height for a man but tall for a woman. She was carrying more weight than he remembered, but she still looked good in her mid-fifties. Light skinned damn near red skin complexion hence the nickname Pepper Red. Her hair was in crochet braids and looked like fire-red yarn. She stepped in, walking around the place, taking it all in.

"Like the sign out front."

"Thanks."

"I see you got help too."

"You heard about Parker?"

"That boy you used to run around with, it was three of you, no, not him. I'm talking about the little white boy pulling the lawnmower out from around back."

Black went outside to find the boy pouring gasoline into the lawnmower. "What are you doing?"

"Earning my keep, I see the grass ain't cut in a while, I'll do the front and back, and we'll call it even. I'll clean the grass and return the mower where I found it."

Black wanted to scold the boy for breaking into his garage but needed to see what his mother wanted. He nodded at the boy and returned inside, closing the door behind him.

"You been to see Pops?"

"Yeah, I saw the old man; he still ain't got rid of that old house."

"What are you doing back here Pepper Red?"

"Need to settle some old debts."

"It's been over twenty years, ma."

"When the debt collector comes, you have to pay no matter how long it's been."

"I'm guessing you came to say hi, handle your business, then bounce back out of town?"

"Something like that came to hire you."

Black laughed. "Stop playing, ma."

She reached into a backpack and removed two bundles of rolled-up hundred-dollar bills wrapped in rubber bands. She extended the money. Black grabbed her by her wrist and examined the tattoo. He recognized the symbol;

it was a figure eight on its side. The infinity symbol signifies the concept of eternity.

"What's this?"

She yanked her arm away, ignoring his question. "Need you to find a man."

"What man, for what?"

"Either to clear my name or to kill him. Either way, this ends before I leave Chicago."

***

CHAPTER THREE

Black sets a coffee mug with a teabag in front of his mother. He removes a tea kettle and pours the steaming hot water into the cup, pours himself a cup, and joins her at the counter.

"Start this from the beginning Pepper Red."

She dips her tea bag in and out of the water. "I'm sure you've heard all the stories from your daddy and his side of the family."

"You want me to take the case? This is how I work; treat me as if I don't know."

She pulled the bag from the cup and set it on a saucer near her cup. She picked up a teaspoon and began spooning sugar into her cup. "Fine, Gerald Eggleston."

"Lil G Man?"

"Yes, Lil G Man back in the day came up under his uncles Frank and Willie Eggleston. Was heavy in the game in the late '60s and early '70s used to move Heroin on the West Side up to Cicero."

"Okay."

"When the '80s rolled around, I like to think people started picking sides."

"Picking sides?"

"Yeah, that's what I called it; we were teenagers doing grownup shit, so that's the age you decide what side you are going be on- some went off to join the army, some got jobs at the post office like your daddy, had a few guys I knew whose uncles were into roofing, so they went to work with them. A very small few went off to college. Then you had the knuckleheads that ended up junkies. Or the girls that either got knocked up and got on the welfare or got knocked up and married."

Black took a sip from his cup. "Which were you?"

She laughed. "I was in my category." Black raised an eyebrow, and she continued. "Let's just say I was a Jane of all trades. I married your daddy, did the college thing for a while, had you, and dabbled in the game a little bit."

"Dabbled a little bit, huh?'

She laughed. "Alright, I won't say a little bit; let's say I dabbled more than most."

"And amid that dabbling?"

"I stepped out on your daddy; this was before the days of DNA testing, so your daddy never admitted it, but I always felt he had doubts about your sister being his."

Black sat stone-faced. She continued. "He never said a word, and he loved her much more than he loved me."

"As far as I remember, Pops never mistreated you Pepper Red."

"No, but you're a man now; you've experienced love from a woman and loving a woman, and once the love is gone, the love is gone. He said we could get over it, but I knew he'd always think about Gerald and me."

Black took another sip from his cup and nodded in agreement.

"Don't you want to know?"

"Know what?"

"If Ally was Pope's child."

Black laughed.

"What?"

"Nothing, just haven't heard anyone call Pops by his first name in a long time; he's just Pops to everybody on the block."

"Yeah, well, he's always Pope to me; answer the question."

"No, I don't care who her father was; it doesn't matter; she was my sister no matter what. I would like to know why you didn't pay your respects or haven't seen your grandchild?"

"Who says I didn't?"

"You went to Ally's funeral?"

"With the risk of being killed or arrested, yes, I did."

Black picked up his cup from the counter and placed it on the sink. She continued. "That's how I know you weren't there; you were over in Africa or some shit helping some white chick find her little girl instead of taking care of business with your sister."

"She wasn't white; she was Hispanic."

"Same difference; she ain't Black."

"I'm not doing this with you Pepper Red, and Pops could've told you that."

"He did. When I was at your sister's funeral in Indiana, he told me about that mess in Danville, too; what is it with you and these women?"

"Again, I'm not talking about this with you; you want to get back to Lil G Man?"

"To shorten a long story after your father and I split."

"You ran out on us."

"We separated."

"Same difference."

"Are you telling this story, or am I?"

"Go ahead."

"I mean, damn, I hope you're not rude to all your customers like that."

"My bad Pepper Red, go ahead- after you two split."

"I got a little spot over in Hammond, Indiana."

"Wait, you stayed around?"

"Yeah, right across the border."

"Did Pops know? He made it seem like you were gone-gone."

She shrugged her shoulders. "Pope knew, but I suppose I was gone-gone as you put it in his mind, so he told you what he told you. Around this time, I got heavy into the game."

"Moving weight with Lil G Man?"

"Nah, that's what your daddy people probably told you coming up, but they don't know shit."

"What was it then?"

"You were the former D.A. and studied case law, and I'm guessing you worked on some organized crime stuff in your stint with the prosecutor's office, correct?"

"A little bit, yeah."

"What do you know about some of the hits in Chicago from back in the day?"

Black shrugged his shoulders. "I don't know a little bit here and there- stuff about Capone, the Folks, some about the Black P Stone Nation from back in the day, the Flores twins."

"Answer this for me if you can, then, Mr. historian- a known hitman for the outfit named William Dauber and his wife Charlotte were chased in their car and shotgunned to death after leaving the Will County, Illinois, courthouse. In 83, Japanese Chicago mob boss Ken Eto survived a Mafia hit and testified in court against the Chicago Outfit, sending more than a dozen fellow mobsters and corrupt cops to prison. Two of the triggermen of Eto's failed hit, Jasper Campise and Johnny Gattuso, were later found dead in the trunk of one of their cars. Ronald Terry and his woman Candid Sanders were murdered in his white Cadillac after relocating to Memphis to organize the Vice Lords in Tennessee. Four Corner Hustler Marcus Hurley was fatally shot as he left a convenience store. William (Lil Man) Cartagena, one of the top lieutenants of the Latin Kings here in Chicago, relocated to New York to organize the gangs; there found in an abandoned Bronx apartment strangled, decapitated, mutilated, and his corpse set on fire. What do they all have in common?"

"The hell if I know- Italians, Vice Lords, Four Corner Hustlers, and Latin Kings, what they have in common, they were all part of Chicago organizations?"

"Besides the obvious, son?"

"All murdered?."

"Me, I did all the hits and a lot more that people don't even know about; these are just the highlights."

Black let out an uncomfortable laugh. "Even if I did believe you, which for the record I don't- one, why are you telling me all of this, and two, what does it have to do with Lil G Man?"

"You wanted the truth of why I left Chicago. I was a private contract enforcer. The gangland hits from the '80s and '90s, and I did them. Either they gave the Italians credit or gang bangers." She chuckled. "Hell, let them have the glory. Besides, no one would suspect a woman of pulling off these hits, let alone a Black woman; it kept the heat off of me."

Black leaned against the counter, folded his arms across his chest, and stared into his mother's face. "This is a lot to take in. Did Pops know?"

"He did."

"And he never told me?"

"Why would he? The rumors about me were better than the truth. Anyway, I'm only telling you this because being here is some life-or-death shit; if anything happens to me, you need to know the players involved."

Black nodded that he understood. She continued. "I had a handler that handled getting the jobs and making sure the money was right, a guy named Scat-Man Chatman."

"He owns stepper's clubs from here to Georgia."

"Yes sir, he got me jobs in states all along the Mississippi; when you see him ask him about the job he got me in on in 97."

"Scat-Man can clear your name?"

"I don't know; that's what I hired you for."

"To find Scat-Man?"

'That'll be a good place to start."

"Did you do it Pepper Red?"

"Do what?"

"You know what?"

"Kill Gerald?" Black didn't respond; she continued. "No."

"Wait, back up; you didn't do it? I've been told all my life you killed Lil G Man over him sleeping with another woman."

"I told you; your daddy's people don't know shit."

"What I never understood was why the police suspected you. Even when I was with the D.A.'s office, I couldn't find out; believe me. I tried; the files are sealed."

"That's why I need you to find Big Heart; I got word that he's been released and is staying in Illinois. I have a few connects here putting feelers out around Maywood, where his peoples stay, but nothing has surfaced yet."

"You think that's a good idea? I've never encountered any of his people, but he still holds weight in the streets and might still want you dead."

"He does; there's still a bounty on my head."

"Why go through this? Dodging people on the street, dodging the police?"

"I'm getting old, tired of living like this worrying about my door being kicked in, and the answers to this might start with Big Heart."

Black pulled up a chair and took his mother's hands into his. "Let's take a step back from this for a second." She inhaled, then exhaled. He continued. "Where have you been all this time Pepper Red?"

"When I first got the wire that there was a warrant for my arrest of Lil G Man's murder, I just barely missed getting pinched, mashallah, wallahi."

Black smiled. He hadn't heard the Islamic phrase of thankfulness in a while. She continued. "Got out the state, drove to Wisconsin, hid out at one of Scat-Man's stepper lounges until he came through with some fake IDs and passports from some S.A.'s he knew caught me a one-way flight to Algiers. I used the money I saved and paid for safe passage and political asylum. Things were good for a while; I was having Scat-Man get money to Pope for you and your sister, and I was adjusting to life in a foreign country. I was learning Arabic and teaching painting classes; then, things got funky. A new regime of politicians came into power and wanted more money for me to stay there. I told them I needed time to get the funds but figured they might take the money and turn me over to the United States authorities anyway or keep asking for more money whenever they felt like it, so I returned to the States. Money was running low, and I couldn't risk taking jobs, so I converted to a citizen's life under the radar as much as possible and moved to Memphis for a while, taking jobs that paid under the table. I didn't stick around long. Next, I spent some time in Arkansas. Hit the West Coast, landed in Vegas, got a job as a cook at a hotel, headed home one night, got pulled over and taken in did a weekend in Clark County luck was on my side got out after a 72-hour hold for some reason my prints didn't hit with the F.B.I. database. I immediately caught a cab from the jail to a Greyhound station, got my ass off the West Coast, got a ticket to Detroit, stayed a year or two, then backtracked to Little Rock, and been staying there ever since."

"Well damn, Pepper Red did you leave anything out?"

"I'm sure I did."

Black gave his mother a disappointed look. She squeezed his hand. "It's nothing to do with this mess, and I promise you that."

He placed her hand on his lips and kissed the back of her hand. "That was a lot to unload; we'll get started in the morning. You can stay with me."

She shook her head no. "No, I'm still on the wanted list." She reached into her bag, removed a cell phone, and slid it across the counter to Black. "I'll reach you on this, a burner." Black picked up the phone, looked at it, and nodded in agreement.

***

CHAPTER FOUR

U p early the following day, Black rolled out of bed, stretched, dropped to the floor, and did two hundred push-ups; showered, dressed in a black tank top covered by a silk black collared button-up, black slacks, and black hard-bottom dress shoes. He grabbed a cranberry-orange muffin and a protein shake and was out the door. Pulling out of his underground garage in his Black Jaguar XJ, his Walther P99 sat on his lap as he headed towards the highway going North to Glenview.

When he got home last night, he couldn't sleep. It was a lot to take in that his mom was back. He didn't think about her often; he had already accepted that he would probably never see her again and was okay with that. If she was on the run and alive and free, knowing that was better than him being able to see her behind bars no matter what she did, she was still his mother.

Instead of lying awake in bed, he did a few quick internet searches and looked up some of the names his mother had given him. He would start with Scat-Man, real name Satchel Chatman, and see where that leads him.

Forty minutes later, he was getting off Lake Ave in Wilmette; he followed the GPS directions until reaching the address he was looking for. It wasn't hard to find his address online; he looked up his businesses and the Articles of Organizations with the State. Black got lucky he had it listed under his home address. Many small companies operated this way. Black was surprised that an operation of his size still had it set up this way. Whatever the reason, it worked in his favor. He let his Jag idle a few houses down from the address he was looking for. He watched the house for twenty minutes before placing his gun in front of his pants and covering it with his shirt. He turned the car off, got out, and walked up the street to the house he had been watching.

Black noticed the Ring doorbell, a new form of home security that was all the new rage now. With a doorbell system with a camera built into it, it would be hard-pressed to find a home that didn't have one. Black winked at the camera and then knocked on the door. Within seconds the door was opened, and staring back at Black was a man at least twenty years his senior, what the women would call a silver fox.

Gray dreadlocks resting on his shoulders, he answered the door bare-chested. He wore a pair of Adidas track pants and matching Adidas sandals. The gray beard and chest hair matched his dreadlocks. His chest, shoulders, and arms were Jacked, his midsection not so much; he had a small pudge. He was neck to neck in height to Black.

He stared Black in the eye through hazel eyes. "What can I do for you?"

"I'm looking for a Satchel Chatman."

"I'm Satchel, and you are?"

"My name is Black Love, and I'm a private investigator. If that's alright, I'd like to ask you a few questions."

"Love?" Pepper Red's boy?"

Black nodded. Scat-Man stepped to the side and allowed him to come in. Once inside Scat-Man closed the door behind him. Black surveyed the place; it was a nice-looking home. Black followed behind as he led the way. His living room walls were covered with pictures from dance competitions of him with different women as dance partners; judging by the clothes he was wearing in the photos, it looked like the pictures had been taken over a few decades.

In many of the pictures, he was holding trophies. In other pictures, he posed with celebrities: Don Cornelius, Bishop Magic Don Juan, Pam Grier, Bootsy Collins, and Lynda Carter. When they finally reached the living room, he had an entertainment center dedicated to nothing but trophies from different dance competitions that he'd won.

His furniture was nothing fancy, a black leather sofa and a loveseat combo. He had a flatscreen tv hanging on the wall, tuned to YouTube, and Ohio Players, played on the television. He motioned for Black to sit as he flopped down on the sofa, and Black copped a squat across from him on the loveseat.

"How Pepper Red been?

"I couldn't tell you."

Scat-Man raised an eyebrow and shook his head skeptically. "What can I do for you?" He asked as he removed a pack of Top's cigarette rolling papers from his pocket and placed them on a glass table before him.

"Wanted to know what you could tell me about a job back in 97."

Scat-Man chuckled as he pulled a glass plate filled with blue-hued weed in front of him. He grabbed the buds, stuffed them into a weed grinder, and began twisting. "97, that's a long time ago. I remember he used to brand his broads, man, that dude was something else."

Black didn't respond. Scat-Man sat the grinder on the table next to the Tops. He leaned back into the leather, ran his fingers through his hair, and exhaled. "Why do you want to go digging all this stuff up?"

"Someone asked me to look into it as a favor."

Scat-Man picked up the rolling papers and pulled two sheets from the pack. Holding the sheets between his pointer finger and middle finger, he pointed at Black.

"You should tell that friend to let sleeping dogs lie."

"All the same, Mr. Chatman, sir, I'd like to know the answer."

"Pepper Red wouldn't want you digging this old stuff up, son."

"I'm not your son, and you don't speak for my mother and what she would want. Are you going to tell me about the job or what?"

Scat-Man picked up the grinder, opened it, and took his time rolling the marijuana into the two Top's papers he stuck together. "Back in 97, you say?" Black nodded. Scat-Man licked the joint, removed a Bic lighter from his pocket, placed the joint between his lips, lit it, took a pull, and blew out the smoke. "Alan Archibald, folks used to call him Westside Willie, don't ask me why. Been dead for over 30 years now. If I remember shit, that was the year Lil G-Man bit it."

Scat-Man offered the joint to Black, but Black declined. Scat-Man crossed one leg over the other and took another pull. "You answer me, young blood, why this person who hired you even cares about some shit from a hundred years ago?"

Black stood and placed his hands in his pockets. "It's like I said, I was hired to find out some information, that's it, that's all."

"She do the job?"

"She says she didn't."

"But..."

"He dead, ain't he?"

"You think she did it?"

"I think it ain't none of my business and ain't none of this going bring G Man back, and it ain't going get your mama off the FBI's wanted list."

"Why did someone want Lil G Man dead?"

Scat-Man stood. "Not in the why business, some cat wants another cat's clock punched, and he has the paper to get it done the why don't make me no, never mind."

"If you had to guess."

"Not in the guessing business either."

"Look, man, I'm just trying to get to the bottom of this, not looking to get you jammed up."

Scat-Man chuckled. "Youngblood, I ain't worried about you; if it weren't for your mama, I would've put one in your forehead for asking me these questions. I don't know you from Adam."

Black smirked. Scat-Man pulled a Glock .43 from the pocket in his track pants and pointed it at Black's stomach.

"Like I said, just trying to get some things cleared up."

"And as I said, you lucky you Pepper Red's boy, our little Q&A session is done." Scat-Man motioned with the gun. "Go on; you remember the way."

Black started walking back the way he entered until he was back outside in his car, pulling off.

***

CHAPTER FIVE

A little storefront nestled between a bakery and a Chinese restaurant at 3040 S. Kedzie housed the Major Crimes base of operations—a four-person unit run by Special Detective Pat Bosselait. Bosselait, a 6'11, 350 lbs., blonde-haired, Nordic-looking white guy with a crooked nose, had been running the unit for almost two decades. He sat at his desk, going through files, trying to decide who their next target would be.

His second in command, Special Detective Yvonne Wu, Asian, under 5'5, thin frame, wore her hair in a pixie cut, had freckles, and wore thin wired glasses. She was looking over travel brochures at her desk. Across the room, the other two detectives played one-on-one basketball with the hoop stationed in the office during downtime.

The door opened, and the sun from outside briefly shined in before the door slammed closed again with a loud thud. No one stopped what they were doing, and didn't get visitors other than Commander Mari Melendez. She marched into the headquarters, not acknowledging the men playing ball as they both yelled their hellos to her as she continued towards Bosselait. Upon reaching his desk, she nodded at Wu, who nodded back and then dropped a file on Bosselait's desk.

"Your next case."

Bosselait didn't look up from the case file he was already going through. "If you didn't notice, Commander, we already have a shit load of cases; pass it on to another unit.

Melendez is standing at 5'0 feet herself, with a golden brown skin tone and hair down her back. If it weren't for her gun and badge fastened to her belt, you wouldn't know she was a cop. She smelled of Boadicea, the Victorious Blue Sapphire perfume, almost $1,000 a bottle. Givenchy leather calf-high boots and matching Givenchy dresses or pants suits were her usual attire. Today she wore a black Asymmetric pleated skirt with a bandana pattern, and a matching black bandana wrapped fashionably around her hair; Dolce & Gabbana sunglasses covered her face.

"Did anything I said sound like it had a question mark hanging at the end of it?"

Bosselait sat the file down and picked up the one she placed on his desk. "No, it did not, Commander." He tossed the file to Wu, and it landed on her desk. She picked it up and began reading it. "You wanted to run an OP on your own, have at it, Wu; you run this one." He picked the file he was looking at back up and began reading again. "What makes this case so special anyway? You know this being a special unit and all."

Melendez removed her sunglasses. "It's a body in Englewood; an abandoned house got called in this morning."

Bosselait sighed. "Great, now we're taking on Homicide's slack too."

"This one's coming from the Deputy Chief."

Bosselait peeked over the file he was looking at and locked eyes with Melendez. "No, shit?"

"No shit."

"In Englewood? What, some rich kid get caught on the wrong side of town?"

"Nope, some mid-level veteran dealer ran with a strong crew back in the late 90s, but recently he's been in and out Joliet for the past two decades, moves a few ounces here and there, nothing major."

Bosselait stood and walked around to Wu's desk, stood behind her, trying to read over her shoulder. She tilted her head and frowned. "You mind? You know I hate that shit."

Bosselait laughed as he took two steps back. "Alright, alright, give me the highlights."

Wu began reading. "Larry Rucker, male, Black, six feet even, two-hundred forty pounds, 58 years of age, divorced, two-time loser, both times he did a little over a nickel at Joliet. Both times for possession of a narcotic with intent to distribute. I'm guessing a handful of arrests petty thefts in his earlier days, catch and release because he did no real-time on those."

"I'm still not hearing anything, major Commander...you know Major Crimes, right?"

"Don't give me shit, Bosselait; the Deputy Chief wants it done fast and right, no loose ends." She placed her glasses on her face and returned to where she came in. "And clean this place up; open a window or something; it smells like a frat house." She opened the door and stepped out, and it slammed closed behind h er.

"Were you serious, boss? I get to run this one the way I see fit?"

"Hell yeah, you know I like my prey with meat on the bones, and what did you say his name was?"

"Larry Rucker."

"Yeah, Larry Rucker, he has no meat on his bones."

"Thanks, boss." She continued reading. "Known associates: Gerald "Lil G Man" Eggleston, uncles Frank and Willie Eggleston, William "Big Heart" Mossberry. Do any of those names ring a bell?"

"Nope, you did say he's been in the game a while, all before my time."

"What about a Sharon Miner Mohamed?"

He whistled across the room and held his hands up. One of his detectives launched the basketball at him, and he caught it and shot for the basket from across the room. He missed; it bounced off the backboard, and one of the detectives caught it. "Nope, never heard of her. Is she Middle Eastern?"

"African American female, she's been on the Most Wanted list since the 90's known relatives still here in Chicago: ex-husband one Pope Love, two children, a daughter Ally Love deceased, and son-"

"Black Love." He said, cutting her off and snatching the file out of her hands. "Now him I've heard of, son of a bitch."

Wu crossed her arms across her chest. "I take it this will be our next case?" He didn't respond. She continued. "And I will not be the lead on this one either?"

He began walking towards the door. "That's why you're my right-hand man Wu; you're with me; you two hold down the fort until we get back."

***

CHAPTER SIX

P ops sits on the side of the bed in a hotel room in South Beloit, WI wearing only a white tank top, matching boxers, and white socks. Pepper Red lies with her head in his lap, and he runs his fingers through her hair.

"Sharon, you know you are still beautiful as ever."

She smiled. "You got old."

He pinched her nose, and they both laughed. He leaned down and kissed her nose. "Still mean as ever too."

She rose from his lap, sat beside him, and laid her head on his chest.

"Will any of this ever be over, Sharon?"

"One way or another."

He sighed. "It wasn't worth it to come back. You can get in that car and drive back to where it was you've been and never look back."

She stood from the bed, picked up her pants from the floor, and slid them on. "Don't do that, Pope."

"Do what?"

"That thing you do when you try to tell me what's best for me."

Pops stood and grabbed Pepper Red's shoulders. "As long as God pumps air in my lungs, you'll be my wife."

She smiled and kissed him on the lips. "I love you for that, Pope, always will, and in some ways, I'll always be your wife. I couldn't change that if I wanted to, like I can't change who I am if I wanted to." She reached around him underneath the pillow on the bed, grabbed her gun, checked the chamber, and placed it in the front of her pants.

Pops began getting dressed. Silence hung in the room like a mist. "What now?" he asked as they both approached the door.

"We hug, kiss, and go our separate ways until we meet again in another twenty years." She laughed and stood stone-faced. She wrapped her arms around his neck, still laughing. "I knew I shouldn't have given you none; after all these years, you still pout when mama gotta leave."

He wrapped his arms around her waist. "Still an asshole after all these years."

She locked her lips with his in a passionate kiss. "You love my attitude; that's why you married me."

"Sharon, things get too heavy for you to carry; call me."

"Don't worry, Pope."

He stared into her eyes. "I'm not playing with you, woman."

She pushed him in the chest. "I hear you, old man; dang, you used to be more fun; you got so cranky."

He opened the door for her, and as she stepped out, he slapped her across the butt, and it stung, but she smiled.

Once outside, Pops got into his car and pulled out of the lot. She hopped into hers and drove in the opposite direction. Lost in her thoughts, she hadn't noticed a car following her.

***

CHAPTER SEVEN

B lack navigated the Black Jaguar XJ and got off on Stoney Island. Headed towards 103rd was on his way to the 4th district to meet Detective "Bunchy" Edwards, a missing person's detective. They had worked on a few cases together previously, Black needed background checks, and since his regular hacker Seshat was M.I.A., he would have to squeeze a favor out of Bunchy. The police station wasn't one of his favorite places to go; his history with Captain Roberts wasn't good, and he and Black never meshed for one reason or another.

Black stepped from the elevator into the Missing Person's Department; no one paid any particular attention to him as he moved through the office looking for Bunchy's desk. He spotted him on a phone call. From the little that Black heard, it sounded as if he were arguing with his wife; at least, that's what Black guessed he didn't know for sure he could only faintly hear a woman's voice yelling. Black stood silently near his desk. When Bunchy noticed him, he ended the call.

"Have a seat, Love; last favor, I don't need to be on the captain's bad side. Let's get you out of here. Who are we looking up?"

"Alan Archibald."

Bunchy keyed in the name, and a few seconds later, an arrest record popped up. Bunchy moved the mouse around the screen, and the printer across the room came to life and started spitting out paper.

"Thanks. Can you see if there is a list of known associates or next of kin?"

Bunchy tapped the keyboard again until another list appeared, moved the mouse, and printed more pages. "Anything else?"

"Nah, that's it."

Bunchy got up and went to the printer to retrieve the pages. He returned and handed them to Black. "How's the private sector been treating you? Money been good?"

"Why you ask, looking to give the badge up?"

Bunchy shook his head no. "Nah, I was wondering if you needed any help around the office with anything. Joanne needs a job, and she has me around here pulling my hair out." Joanne was his daughter. Once a runaway, Black helped find her and bring her back home. Black laughed. "How is she, you know, since she's been back home?"

"I thought everything would be cool, and it was for about a day."

"A day?"

Bunchy chuckled. "Alright, a week. I'm not too fond of the path she's going down. I can be heavy-handed on the discipline side of parenting, which makes her act out more; that's what made her run off the first time, and we both know how that turned out."

"Let me think about it. I'll reach out if I can do anything."

Bunchy nodded, and Black reached out his hand for a handshake.

"Thanks again for the search. I'll be in touch.

***

CHAPTER EIGHT

Black sat in his car down the street from Harold's Chicken on S. Halsted, eating his chicken and fries with Mild Sauce. Licking his fingers, he thumbed through the printouts he got from Bunchy. Westside Willie had been dead for a while now and said he had a wife back in the day named Ilene Archibald, it would be a long shot, but he would see if he could track her down by the old address they had on file. Before he keyed in the address, he typed her name into Facebook and Instagram to see if anything would pop up. When nothing did, he finished the last piece of chicken and headed towards the address on file.

Black crept into the neighborhood; not many people gave him a second look as he parked across the street from the house he was looking for; Black checked his gun in the front of his pants and got out, closed the door, pressed the alarm, and locked the doors as he made his way to the house. He nodded at the kids playing in front of the house. Black stepped on the porch and knocked on the screen door. The front door was open; he could see into the home. He knocked again as a girl who looked to be no older than twelve came to the door.

"Hello, I'm looking for a Mrs. Ilene Archibald."

"My grandma? It ain't Archibald; it's Johnson." The girl turned her head and yelled. "Mama, some man at the door asking for grandma!"

"Girl, get away from that damn door!" Black heard the voice yell as the girl turned and walked away; a few seconds later, he heard feet coming his way; he assumed it was the mother who appeared before him.

"Hello, I'm a private investigator named Black Love. Does an Ilene Archibald live here?"

"Yes, Ilene Johnson is my mother; she hasn't gone by Archibald in years. What are you looking for, my mother?"

"I'm conducting an investigation, and Alan Archibald's name came up; she was once his wife, wasn't she?"

She laughed. "That's a name I haven't heard in a long time. I thought Westside Willie was dead?"

"He is. That's why I'm here. Is Ms. Johnson home?"

"You have some type of ID or something?"

Black patted his pockets and removed his wallet, opened it, and removed a private investigator's card, and he held it up to the screen so that she could read it. She nodded, he took a step back, and she opened the screen door. He stepped i n.

"Have a seat here, and I'll go and get Mama, see if she feels like talking."

Black nodded and sat on the sofa. It wrapped around the small living room; it was a leather sectional.

"Lil girl, go get our guest a drink." He heard the woman yell from another room. He looked around the place, it smelled like lemon pledge, and the scent made him look down at the floor—all wood, shining as if it had just been polished. Besides the leather sectional, there was a 72-inch flat-screen hanging on the wall, an old school record player sat in the corner of the room, and stacked against the wall were crates of old records. A few seconds later, the little girl who answered the door appeared carrying a bottle of Corona beer, a lime sitting on the top of the bottle. Black accepted the bottle.

"Thank you."

"You're welcome." Then once again, she was gone.

Black pushed the lime into the bottle and began guzzling the cold drink. He heard feet shuffling across the floor, moving at a plodding pace; he assumed it was Ms. Johnson, and a few moments later, she appeared before him. She was shorter than he, maybe 5'0, and looked like she weighed a hundred pounds. Gray hair flowing down her back uncombed. She wore a pink Nike jogging suit and house shoes. Black stood to greet her.

"Hello, Ms. Johnson, I'm Black Love, thanks for taking the time to talk to me."

She waived him off. "Go on, sit down; no call for all of that."

Black smiled and sat. She made her way to an EZ chair across from him in front of the television; she swiveled the chair to sit face-to-face with him. "I don't know what I can tell you about Alan."

"Whatever you can remember will help tremendously."

"Alright."

"You need anything, mama?"

"Bring me a glass of that lemonade, baby."

"Yes, ma'am, Mr. Love, anything else for you?"

"No, ma'am, and thank you for the beer."

She nodded and was off. Black scooted to the edge of his seat to get closer to Ms. Johnson. "I wanted to know if you knew if any of the people that Alan Archibald used to run with were still alive. Maybe a relative or something?"

She laughed. "Alan never had many friends, ladies; now that's a different story. Cheating bastard." Black chuckled. She continued. "You married Mr. Love?"

"No, ma'am."

"A girlfriend...excuse me, don't want to assume you are just into girls. You got a shim?"

Black's face wrinkled in confusion just as her daughter returned with the lemonade and handed it to her mother. She giggled.

"Behave yourself, mama." She turned and faced Black. "A shim is what Mama calls gay men, and she and him...a shim."

Black shook his head and smiled. "No, ma'am, no shims or anything other than women, and no, I don't have a girlfriend either."

"Well, get all your screwing out your system before you get yourself one; it makes no sense to have some woman hanging on to you if you are just going stick your dipstick in and out different oil pans."

"Mama, I said behave. I'm sorry, Mr. Love."

"I'm your mother; you're not mine; you don't tell me to behave."

She shook her head. "I'm sorry, Mr. Love, mama, just be nice."

She took another sip from her glass. "I am nice shit. I ain't telling the man nothing wrong. Go on with the rest of your questions, young man."

Black cleared his throat. "Yes, I was asking if you knew if his friends or relatives were still alive?"

"Alan never had much family, not in Chicago anyway; his peoples were from down south. I knew he had a brother on his daddy's side; outside children were common in those days, hell is common now. What about you, Mr. Love you have a bunch of outside children?"

"No, ma'am, no kids at all."

"What's the matter? You got that E.D.....was watching a show on Dr. Phil; they were talking about that, you know when the men can't get it up."

The daughter placed her hand on her face in embarrassment. "I'm going to let you two have some privacy."

"Don't run off, shit we all grown, don't act like you ain't been with a man whose soldier couldn't salute."

"I am not talking about this with you, mama, Mr. Love; just yell when you're ready to leave."

Black nodded. He faced Ms. Johnson. "If we can get back to the questions about Alan, ma'am, this brother, would you remember his name?"

"Now that brother, that's the one I should have picked; he was fine-fine...that's what the young folks saying, ain't it?"

Black laughed. "Yes, ma'am."

She shrugged her shoulders. "He probably was worse than Alan, the fine ones always having a slew of women and even more children all over town. Anyway, the brother's name was Larry Rucker, I haven't seen him since Alan, and I broke up decades ago don't know if he's still around or not."

"You wouldn't happen to have an address, would you?"

"You know it's funny you ask; no, I don't have an address, but his mama, God bless her soul, was going to my church before she passed. I know she used to live on 64th and King Drive, I don't know if she still got people around there, but I suppose it's a good place to start."

"Thank you, ma'am."

"Umm, hmm. Now let me ask you some questions."

Black smiled. "Go ahead."

"You have something against children?"

"No, ma'am, why would you ask that?"

"Just wanted to know. What about my daughter?"

"What about her?"

"You like her?"

"I barely know her being that we just met today."

"No, I mean, do you like her? She fine, ain't she?"

Black laughed and stood to his feet. "Yes, ma'am, she's lovely."

"You are short for her taste but more professional than the type she ends up with. She works, helps take care of me, does alright with them children; they ain't too misbehaved."

"Yes, ma'am."

"You should ask her out."

Her daughter stepped into the room just as she said it, and a flash of embarrassment again covered her face. "Mama cut it out. I do just fine meeting men on my own."

"The hell you do." She stood to her feet and extended her hand to Black. "Help me outside."

"What are you doing, mama?"

"I want to sit on my porch; I ain't got to ask permission to sit on my porch."

Black took her by the arm and guided her towards the door. The daughter held the door open as the two stepped out. There was a folding chair sitting on the porch. Black helped her into the chair, and she held onto his hand. "Think about it, honey; she's a good woman."

Black looked up at her daughter, who was standing in the doorway. "I'll do that, ma'am. Thank you for answering my questions; meeting you was a pleasure."

***

CHAPTER NINE

Black returned to his office; he didn't have any real business to tend to at the office but liked to make his presence felt in the community, so he stopped at least once daily. It wasn't long at the office before there was a knock at the door. Black opened the door to find the white kid from the day before; this time, he wasn't alone. A stocky, average, height guy with prison tattoos and a buzz cut stood beside him.

"What can I do for you, kid?" Black said, addressing the young man.

The boy didn't answer; the stranger spoke up. "You see this kid before?"

"I have."

"Do you and me a favor; he comes around here again, you send him to me, and I set him straight. Let him know he's not welcome around these parts; you don't have to worry about him bothering you again."

"Excuse me, you are?"

"This is my Uncle Mickey."

Mickey backhanded the boy across the face. "Shut your mouth when adults are talking."

The boy held his face. Mickey continued. "He says you paid him for some work yesterday?"

"I did."

"I didn't believe how he got it; you know how boys can be when out on their own in the streets."

"Look, you two want to come in and talk-"

Mickey placed his hand on his nephew's shoulder. "No need, that's all I wanted to say-"

"Well, what do we have here? Mickey Sikora and Black Love."

Mickey didn't turn around; he knew the voice oh too well. Black recognized the voice as well. He looked past Mickey and the boy to see Detective Bosselait and his partner approaching; she stopped a few feet back he walked up to the door. He continued. "When did you two start doing business? I didn't know the Mick's liked mixing it up with the brothers."

"Fuck off," Mickey said as he guided the boy away from the building. "Get in the car," Mickey said to his nephew.

"We'll chat later, Mickey," Bosselait said as he stood face to face with Black. "Aren't you going to invite me in?"

"Why would I? We don't have any business to discuss."

"Oh, I think we do."

"Nah, we don't, not after that bullshit you pulled that got Parker violated back."

"That was a raw deal, can't go around striking officers, especially when on parole."

"Well, Parker made of better stuff than I am because he said that ass whooping he put on you was worth going back for."

Bosselait let out an uncomfortable laugh. "Yeah, well, I'm sure he's enjoying himself. The business at hand."

"Would be what?"

"Sharon Miner Mohamed."

"What about her?"

"You see her?"

"Can't say."

"Can't or won't."

Black didn't respond.

"I heard she's back in town."

Black remained silent. Bosselait continued. "Bodies are dropping, and her name is all over them."

"What do you want from me, detective?'

"You hear from mommy; dearest, be sure to give us a ring or tell ya, mama, to do the right thing and turn herself in."

"You have a good day, detective." He took a step back and closed the door.

***

CHAPTER TEN

After dealing with two unexpected guests, Black went to Roseland to see Pops. He pulled in front of the house, walked through the yard, and up the rickety stairs. Black placed his key into the lock and walked in. As soon as he was through the door, Sparkle Pops all-white Pitbull greeted him. Black paused and rubbed behind her ears.

"Hey, girl."

His phone buzzed on his hip, and he answered on the first ring. It was the woman from across the street.

"What's up, Ms. Jones?" "...White and Black, you say?" He laughed. "Yes, ma'am, they are most definitely the police; yes, ma'am, they are not fooling anyone. Let them watch my place. I'm not doing anything wrong. Thanks, ma'am; I'll take care of it."

Black ended the call and moved through the house, going from the living room to the kitchen, finding Pops in his favorite spot, at the kitchen table watching television. He tuned it to the Western Channel, and The Rifleman was on. A bowl of uncooked split peas sat on the table before him, and something was boiling on the stove. Black smelt it when he entered but couldn't place the scent.

"What's up, Pops?"

Black lowered his head and kissed him on the top of his head.

"What's going on, son?"

"Nothing much; what you got going on, on this stove?"

"A lil tripe simmering."

Black frowned his face.

"Don't act like you don't like it; you grew up on good cooking like this."

"We ain't got to eat like that no more, Pops," Black said, laughing.

"Like what? Tripe is good eating."

"It's cow stomach pops."

"And?"

Black continued laughing. "Never mind."

"Your mother been to see you?"

"Yeah, I saw her."

"You be careful dealing with your mother-son."

"I will. How come you didn't tell me about all the stuff Pepper Red was into, Pops?"

"Wasn't my business to tell."

"That's kind of convenient."

"I don't care what you call it; it wasn't my business; she wanted you to know she would have told you. You know now, right?"

"Yes, sir."

"Sharon is the one to tell you, right?"

"Right again."

"Well, alright, you know that stuff about your mother? Did it change how you view her?"

"What you mean I love mama."

"That ain't what I asked you. I say did it change how you view your mother?"

Black paused for a tick or two. "No sir, it didn't. Surprised me, yeah, change my view? Not at all."

"Then what the hell are we talking about?"

Black laughed. "Well, I wanted to ask your opinion about the case."

"Shoot."

"When this is all said and done, will it end well for Mama?"

"It will, now them folks that wronged her, that's another story altogether."

***

CHAPTER ELEVEN

Homicide Detective Matt Craig, a familiar face at Alderman Berber's office, is of average height and skin tone the color of a brown paper bag. He wore suits at least half a decade old, shoes even older, receding hairline, a potted face, and teeth yellowed from years of smoking. The only redeeming physical quality he had was his light grey eyes. Craig and Berber had a love/hate relationship, and they mostly worked with one another out of necessity. Craig marched to his desk and flopped down in the leather chair across from Berber.

"What can I do for you, Alderman?"

"We have a problem."

"Don't we always?"

"This is different."

Craig didn't respond. Berber continued. "Rucker's dead."

"Good, it's about fucking time; surprised he lived this long. I ain't shedding no fucking tears. I promise you that."

"No, not good at all."

"Fuck outta here; since when do you have a sweet spot in your heart for Rucker?"

"Fuck Rucker."

"You didn't call me down here to dick me around, Alderman; spit it out."

"She's back."

"Who, what fucking she?"

Berber squinted his eyes. Craig's mouth slightly dropped open when he realized who the *"she"* was that he was referring to and tilted his head to the side. He continued. "You're kidding me, right?"

"Do I look like I'm fucking kidding?"

"This is good, right?"

"Could be; we play it right."

Craig stood and paced the room. "Jesus Christ, that was a millennia ago, fuck is she doing back? How do you know it's her? Does she know where it is? She came back to get it, right? Did she do Rucker?"

"She's still on the Most Wanted list; whenever known associates of hers kick the bucket or are arrested, my office gets alerted."

"So, you don't know if it was her."

"It was her."

Craig sat back in his seat. "How can you be sure?"

"I'm trying to keep this as quiet as possible, but the more people I include, the more breadcrumbs I lead straight to me if anyone does start digging into the past. When I got the alert, I had a Deputy Chief that owes me a favor or two-run facial recognition through all the traffic cams on the South and West Side to see if he gets a hit."

"Berber."

"Don't worry; I told him to be discreet and get someone he trusts to do it."

"And?"

"He got a hit."

"What's the play? Put it all over the news, sweep the streets, kick in doors, flush her out?

"Nah, that's too noisy, we don't need her talking to anyone but us; the Deputy Chief kicked it over to Bosselait with Major Crimes; you familiar with him?"

Craig shook his head no. "Nah. What do you want me to do?"

"While Bosselait and his team are hunting her down, you can do your own hunting. You remember Scat-Man?"

"Yeah."

"Go rattle his cage; he was her contractor back in the day; there's no way she hasn't gone to see him."

Craig stood. "How far do you want me to go with this?"

"As far as you need to, she owes both of us."

***

CHAPTER TWELVE

He was stepping out of the stepper's lounge on E. 75th, a lady on his arm at 4 a.m. talking and laughing. Scat-Man was caught off guard and smacked with a pistol across the back of the head. Before falling to his knees, he was grabbed by both arms and thrown against the wall. The woman took a step toward the attacker.

"Wait a minute-"

"Mind your business, lady!" The attacker yelled as he holstered his gun, pulled out a badge, and shoved it in the woman's face.

"Chicago PD, step the fuck back!"

The woman took a step back. "You didn't have to pistol-whip him with ya punk ass! Police are always overstepping and shit." She reached into her purse and removed her phone.

"Mind your business, ma'am...and trust me, you do not want to film this; you do not want these problems."

"Man fuck you and those problems; that was my ride. I'm calling an Uber."

The woman began walking away as Detective Craig placed the cuffs on Scat-Man and placed him in the backseat of his car.

***

CHAPTER THIRTEEN

S cat-Man sat on the loveseat in his living room. Craig stood in front of him, holding a hoagy sandwich. Scat-Man held a cold compress to the back of his head where Craig had smacked him with the pistol, and the bleeding was finally beginning to stop.

"What the fuck is all this about?"

"I think you know Scat; where is she?"

"Where's who?"

"You know fucking who, Pepper Red."

Scat-Man threw his hands in the air. "This is what this shit is about? All that extra shit was unnecessary; we go back over thirty years; we could've talked this out nigga."

"Talk it out? I didn't like you thirty years ago, and I don't like you now."

"Fuck you too."

Still holding the hoagy in one hand, he unholstered his weapon with the other hand. "Start telling me some shit I want to hear real fucking soon, or I'm going to eat this sandwich, and you're going to eat one of these bullets." Craig took a bite out of the sandwich. "Fuck! Damn tooth." Craig yelled out in pain.

"See a dentist."

Craig dropped the sandwich on the floor and held his jaw where the pain came from.

Scat-Man spoke again. "Come on, man, dropping shit all on my floor."

"Fuck a dentist and fuck your floor. Get me Pepper Red."

"I ain't seen Pepper Red in decades; why would I know where she is?"

"I heard she was back, and everyone knows that back in the day. You two were joined at the hip."

"That's news to me; if she's back, she hasn't been to see me."

"Bullshit, were you with her when she did, Rucker?"

"Rucker? Larry Rucker?" Scat-Man laughed. "Why the fuck would she come back to off Rucker?"

"I came for answers, and here you are, giving me more questions."

"I don't know what to tell you; I haven't fucking seen her!"

Craig cocked back the gun and placed the barrel underneath Scat-Man's chin.

"I haven't seen her, I swear, but-"

"But what?"

"Her son came to see me, asking questions about the job in 97."

"Yeah, this son of hers, his name?"

"Black, Black Love."

"Get a hold of him."

"And tell him what?"

"Setup a meet with his mother."

"He's not going to go for that, and he told me he hasn't seen her."

"And you believed him?"

"Of course not, but-"

"You and these fucking buts, if you can't get it done Scat-Man, just tell me, and I'll get your mama a black dress."

"I'll get it done, man damn, get that gun out my face."

Craig removed the gun, re-holstered it, and slapped him.

"You try to run; I'm not going to chase you. I'll just put one in your mother's head."

"Ain't nobody going run I said I can do it, I'll do it.

Scat-Man removed his phone and his wallet. He opened his wallet and pulled out Black's business card that he had given him. He dialed Black, and the phone was answered on the first ring.

"Youngblood, this is Scat-Man; I'm ready to meet and tell you what I know if you're still interested."

***

CHAPTER FOURTEEN

N ow in Englewood, looking for the address Ilene Johnson had given him. He pulled his gun and sat it on his lap; riding down 64th and King Drive, he may need it. He circled the block once, looking for a parking spot when there was none. He double-parked in front of the house he was looking for, reached over the backseat, and grabbed his sports jacket. He put it on and slid his gun into the jacket pocket. He got out and left the engine running.

Keeping both hands in his pocket, the one with the gun, he held his finger near the trigger. He approached the porch, and an older woman sat in a chair, maybe mid-forties braids down her back. The first thing he noticed was that she had one leg. Sitting on the stairs, dumping tobacco from a cigar, sat a young boy who looked like he could be a stand-in for Chief Keef in a music video dreads so long Black could barely see his face. Before Black could speak, he was flanked on the right and left by five other guys; they circled him, leaving him no way to go but forward.

"What you want?" The woman asked, passing a bag of weed to the boy on the stairs.

"My name is Black Love; I'm a private investigator looking for a Larry Rucker."

"Yeah, what you looking for, Larry?"

"I have a few questions about a case I'm working on. Is Mr. Rucker available?"

She chuckled. "Yeah, if you can communicate with folks on the other side."

"What?"

"That nigga Larry dead." The young boy said as he continued rolling the weed.

"Sorry for your loss," Black said. "When did this happen?"

"Found him a few days ago." The woman said, and she nodded to a house down the street. "Found him a few houses down in that abandoned house."

"Sorry to hear that."

"Fucked up, right?"

"Indeed, the police tell you anything about who could've done this?"

The group of boys surrounding him all laughed. She continued. "You are joking, right?"

"When was the last time any of you saw Larry alive?"

The boy rolling the weed spoke again. "I saw the nigga Larry the day he got popped messing around in that old house they found his body in, saw some dude and some milf redbone go in before him."

"You tell the police any of this?'

They all laughed again. Black took their laughter as an answer of no. He also figured that the redbone they referred to was likely Pepper Red. He continued.

"Who did Larry used to run with?"

The woman didn't respond. Black reached into his pocket, removed a bankroll, peeled off two one-hundred-dollar bills, and handed them to the woman.

"Not sure who he ran with, but he had a sister out in Harvey."

"Got an address?"

She eyed Black with a sinister smile; he peeled another hundred dollars off and gave it to her.

"Apartment building on Turlington Ave."

Black placed the money back into his pocket and removed a business card; he extended it toward the woman.

"Do me a favor; if the police tell you anything you think might be important, reach out to me, and I'll pay for any pertinent information you might have."

The woman took the card. "I'll take your card, but I doubt I'll call with anything."

"Thank you, and again sorry for your loss."

"Black."

"Yeah."

"That your real name?"

"Yes, ma'am."

"Next time, Black, I wouldn't ride through O Block in a car like that alone; it's not safe."

Black nodded and turned to leave. None of the guys budged; he locked eyes with the boy standing directly before him. Black gripped his gun with his hands now back in his jacket pocket. He didn't want to get in a shoot-out in broad daylight, significantly outnumbered, but if he had to, he would shoot him first. The boy grimaced at Black revealing a gold grill. The woman spoke up.

"He good ya'll let him through."

They followed her directions and parted, allowing him access to his car. He climbed in, closed the door, and sped from the block.

***

CHAPTER FIFTEEN

B lack put his gun in the front of his pants before getting out and going into the building. He was looking for Larry Rucker's sister at the address in Harvey. Black walked down the hall until he found the apartment he was looking for. Black looked down the hall in the direction that he had just come from once more, then tapped on the door. Black placed his ear to the door to listen to movement. He heard footsteps coming towards the door.

"Who is it?"

"Black Love, I'm looking for a Vicki Rucker."

When the lock turned, and the door opened, standing on the other side of the door was a short round woman. Black didn't know her bosom size, but if he had to guess, it had to be in the triple range; they hung down to her knees. She wore a Mariah Carey t-shirt and, cut-off shorts, dirty flip-flops.

"I'm Vicki."

"I'm Black Love, a private investigator. May I come in?"

A rottweiler came to the door and began growling at Black. Black stared back at the dog, fists and jaws both clenched.

"Go sit your ass down!" Vicki barked the order at her dog as the pet lowered her head, turned, and lay in the middle of the floor.

Black hesitated. He looked around her into the apartment.

"Don't act like a little bitch; you don't have to be scared; ain't nothing going happen to you in here; you wanted information about Larry, right?"

"Yeah."

"Then come on in, scary ass little nigga."

Black ignored the insult and stepped inside. Vicki locked the door behind them and led Black into the living room. Sitting on the floor in front of the plasma tv on the wall playing a video game were two boys looking to be nine and ten in age. Vicki picked up the remote from the couch and turned the television off

.

"Y'all go outside and play until I call y'all inside."

"Dang ma, I was in the middle of that game."

The mother cut her eyes at the boys; they both lowered their heads, rose from the floor, and dashed for the door. Black looked around the apartment as he heard the door open and close.

"A drink?"

Black shook his head no.

"Have a seat."

Black sat on the beige-colored sofa, and she sat next to him. She continued. "Before he was killed, Larry told me he was going to meet a woman."

"What woman?"

"Didn't say."

She reached underneath the sofa and removed an old, tattered photo album. She opened the book and began flipping through the book. "Larry said if I don't hear from him in a few days, call the police."

"I'm not the police."

"No shit. So, I figured it was bullshit because knowing how Larry was, ain't no way he wanted someone to call the police, know what I mean?"

"I do."

"But only it wasn't bullshit, you know after I find out someone killed him."

"And you're sure he didn't tell you who he was meeting or what it was about?"

"No, never told me who or what, but if I had to guess."

"If you had to guess what?"

She stopped looking through the photo album and looked up at Black. "Before I tell you this, I need to know that you'll look out for me."

Black reached into his pocket and removed the bankroll.

She shook her head no. "Nigga that ain't no money."

"What are you talking about then?"

"Give me your word first."

"Nope, not agreeing to something before I know what it is."

She sighed. "For the past decade, I've been hearing Larry complaining about a job he was in on and him getting jerked out his cut."

"What kind of job?"

Vicki handed the photo album to Black; he placed it on his lap and noticed an old yellowing newspaper clipping.

"Chicago's First National Bank robbery...this is from 1997."

"The police never recovered the money or caught any suspects...twenty million dollars cash, in today's time that would...."

"About thirty-five million dollars."

"Yes, sir."

"And Larry had something to do with this job?"

"Damn, you slow; you sure you're a detective?"

"Listen, lady, be cool with all that slick shit."

"Instead of contacting the police with this, I'm contacting you. I figure you a detective and shit you can detect some shit and find that money, give me Larry's cut, and you keep the rest."

"And why would I do that?'

"See, this that shit I was talking about. I knew you would try to fuck me."

"Calm down, and no one's trying to fuck you. I have no intentions of going on some wild goose chase looking for money that A. doesn't belong to me and B. money that's probably spent. What you got other than this newspaper clipping?"

"Flip the page."

Black flipped the page, and next to another newspaper clipping in the book was a crinkled 1997-era hundred-dollar bill.

"Is that from the robbery?"

"He says it is."

"Then where's the rest?"

"Don't know, he said. They were all giving a little walking around money as a part of the plan until the heat died down. According to Larry, they should have washed the money before spending it. They didn't have much think he told me five grand a piece, he washed all of it, but that single hundred-dollar bill said it was the biggest job he ever was a part of and wanted something to remember the day."

"He didn't say who was holding the money. Who was a part of the crew?"

She shook her head no. "Never said, only said the one holding the money was dead and the only person who might know was the dead guy's uncle, only he was doing time in the FEDs, and he claimed he didn't know either."

Black flipped to another page of the book and pointed at the photo.

"Who is this?"

She leaned over and looked closer at the photograph.

"That there is Larry and some of his friends from back in the day."

"I won't sugarcoat this, what you have given me is a step in the right direction, but without any other information, I don't think I can help."

"Look, I'm stepping out on faith with this one Mr. Black Love. Take the hundred-dollar bill and the photo, if you can't find the money maybe you can find who did that to Larry. He wasn't much of a man but was still my brother."

"Yes, ma'am, not making any promises about the money, but if I find out anything about any of this, I'll let you know."

***

CHAPTER SIXTEEN

Veronica Malone felt like she was born for politics; she once felt the same about law enforcement, then about practicing law, and now this. Perhaps she was right about all the above. She thought to herself being Attorney General held elements of all three. She had an already over-stacked schedule she knew she would never get through, and she was, stuffing another appointment into her schedule.

It wasn't as if she even wanted to take the meeting; another part of the job, even after the campaign run is complete and you've won, the games of "playing politics" is never done. She took the meeting as a favor to a colleague of hers. She wanted to turn the meeting down, but favors were currency in Chicago, be it the streets, business, or politics.

So, here she was waiting for an Alderman she only had known by reputation. He was already ten minutes late. She would take this time to write a letter to her boyfriend, Parker. He had been violated back to prison, and she was once conflicted with the dating situation- her being the Attorney General and him being a convicted felon didn't make for good optics. She would give the Alderman until she completed her letter. Then she would have no choice but to move on to the next thing on her agenda. She had hardly gotten into her letter when there was a tap at her door.

"Come in."

Alderman Berber opened the door and stepped in.

"Welcome, Alderman; close the door behind you; please have a seat."

He did as she asked and sat across from her.

"Now, what can I do for you?"

"I must regretfully say that I come with my hands out."

"Oh."

"I know it is in bad form to ask for a favor as soon as meeting someone, but-"

"Here you are. What can I possibly do for you, Alderman?"

"I need an investigation launched into someone."

She picked up her pen and flipped it to a clean page on her notepad. "And what is the individual's name, and what crime do you suspect them of committing?"

"The individual's name is Black Love, and as far as the crime, look under the R.I.C.O. statue. I'm sure something in there can apply to him."

She sets the pen down. "Wait, on what grounds do you want to start an investigation into Black Love, the former District Attorney?"

"As I told you, I think he may be involved in a criminal conspiracy."

Veronica pushed her seat back away from her desk and folded her arms across her chest. "I will need more than that, Alderman, level with me. What's going on here?"

Alderman Berber stood from his seat and looked down at Veronica. "This information doesn't leave this office."

"I'm listening."

"There is a woman by the name of Sharon Miner Mohamed who has been on the Most Wanted list since the 90's we have reason to believe she is back in Chicago."

"And you believe Black Love is helping her?"

"I'd bet my left testicle he's helping her."

"How could you be so sure?"

"Because she's his mother."

Veronica laughed. Alderman Berber remained stone-faced.

"Oh, you're serious."

"Very."

"I'm still lost about the reason for the investigation."

"He's smart and knows the law and all our tactics. We must apply some pressure to help nudge him into doing the right thing. If you get on board with this, it can be career-defining."

Veronica stood. "I'm not going to lie to you, Alderman, I'm not that excited about this proposal, I don't necessarily like the tactics you're trying to apply, but I'm not 100% opposed to them either. I know time is not on our side with this one, but give me by the end of the day to either get back to you with a plan of action or to decline respectfully." She extended her hand for a handshake.

***

CHAPTER SEVENTEEN

After leaving Harvey, he felt a little closer to figuring this thing out. He was glad that Vicki had given him the photo willingly. He wasn't candid with her. Black had recognized one of the people in the photo. He needed to know how much she knew. It made him relax when she couldn't identify anyone from the picture. He held the picture as he sat at a red light staring at the group in the picture posing, staring back with a gangster's demeanor was Pepper Red. The others he didn't recognize but her, he would know anywhere.

He figured it was time to regroup. Time to start from the beginning. Who were the players? At the top of the food chain was his mother, Pepper Red. He had to be objective; was she telling the truth about everything? Was she in on the robbery? He was boxed in by a car behind him and a vehicle in front, cutting him off. Before he could respond, he was pulled from his vehicle, ushered to the back of an unmarked police car, and driven off.

"What the hell is all of this about?" Black demanded as he pulled his cell phone from his pocket.

"Hang it up!" The plainclothes detective demanded without looking into the rearview mirror back at Black.

"The hell I will; this is state-sanctioned abduction; if I am not under arrest, I demand you pull over and let me go now!"

The detective looked up into the mirror and locked eyes with Black. "I said to hang it up!"

The two men had a stare-down; Black hung up as he heard the 9-11 operator speaking through the phone. They pulled into an underground garage, and he shifted to park. With the engine still running, the detective got out, opened the back door, pulled Black from the car, and tossed him to the ground. Black's phone flew from his hands, sliding across the parking lot. Black braced himself for the kick he was sure was about to come. He saw a pair of toned brown legs in heels. His eyes moved past the skirt and blouse until he locked eyes with the person he knew to be in charge. She held out her hand to help him, Blackslapped it away, and rose to his feet.

"What the hell is this all about, Veronica?"

"We need to talk." She began walking back towards her tinted black, bullet-proof Suburban.

"Calling or texting would have been too much, right?"

"What can you tell me about Alderman Berber?"

"Who? The asshole from TV, you tell me he would be more in your social circles than in mine. Why?"

"You two have never crossed paths?"

"No, what the hell is all of this about?"

"What about Sharon Miner Mohamed?"

Black cracked a sly smile. "Now we get to the meat and potatoes of this. You know about my mother. Is that it? You're here to break me, get me to flip on my mother? Well, you're wasting your time; you might as well run me in; I don't know shit, and if I did, you and I both know I wouldn't say."

"Berber never approached you about cooperating with the government to bring your mother in safely?"

"Fuck no. How many ways do I have to say it? I don't know Berber and never met or spoke to him. Where in the hell is all of this coming from?"

"Berber reached out to me personally."

"For what?"

"Launch an investigation against you as leverage to get you to cooperate."

Black held his wrists together as if he was about to be handcuffed. "If that's why you're here, you might as well take me in, not turning on my mother."

"Slow down, put your hands down; that's not why I'm here."

"Why are you here, Veronica?"

"I'm here as a friend to give you a heads up. So, you're sure you don't know why Berber is interested in your mother?"

"Not a clue. Can I go?"

"Why Black?"

"Why what, Veronica?"

"Why do this? Risk everything for a woman that essentially walked out on you?"

"Because she's my mother."

"Not good enough."

"I don't know how you were raised, but-"

"That's right, you don't know, and you don't know her either; you don't owe her shit."

"I'm not doing it for her; I'm doing it for me."

Veronica folded her arms across her chest. "For you?"

Black locked eyes with her. "I have to save her."

Veronica sighed and nodded at her detective. He removed a walkie-talkie radio from his belt and spoke into it. A few seconds later, Black's car pulled into the garage, and another detective got out, leaving the door open. Veronica got into the back of the truck and closed the door. She rolled the window down just as Black got into his car and closed the door. He rolled down his window, and the detective that threw him from the vehicle tossed his cell phone; he caught it.

"I'm putting my neck on the line telling you this, Black, don't let it come back to bite me on the ass."

"I won't," Black said as he shifted into drive and sped from the parking garage.

***

CHAPTER EIGHTEEN

After speaking with Veronica, Black approached the Cook County Medical Examiner's office. He needed answers and wanted to avoid talking with the homicide detective involved in the case if he could. He had no history with this M.E. and had no idea how this would go; he may not help him.

Black walked into the building, and the woman sitting at the front desk he did know. He would need to get past her to gain access to the elevator. Deidre Goodrich, they'd gone on a date or two but didn't mesh. When she kept calling, and he didn't answer, it soured the friendship. Black flashed a smile.

"Hey, Ms. Diedre, how have you been?"

"I'm fine; what do you want, Black?"

Black laughed and placed his hand on top of hers. "Who said I wanted anything but to drop in on an old friend?"

She pulled her hand from his and crossed her arms across her chest. "Umm, hmm."

"Seriously, how are things, seeing anyone?"

She fought it, but it was hard for her to stay mad at Black. She smiled. "You still an asshole."

Black laughed. "I'm a work in progress."

"What you want, Black?"

"I'm a private investigator now, and I'm working a case. I need to get in to see the M.E. help a brother out."

"And what I get out of this?"

"What do you want?"

"I have a shit load of tickets."

"I'm not a police officer, nor the D.A. anymore."

"So, you know people."

Black laughed. "Shit, so do you; look where you work."

"You asked me what I wanted. Can you do it or not?"

"Yeah, I'll make it happen."

"I'm not playing with you, Black; they are talking about putting a boot on my car."

"I got you, girl, straight up."

She unclipped her elevator key card from her blouse and slid it across the counter to Black.

"This will get you downstairs. You have ten minutes, Black; you need to get in and out before the wrong person catches you roaming around down there."

"In and out in a flash; what can you tell me about the M.E.?"

She shrugged her shoulders. "I don't know, skinny little white girl. She's cool, though, and I've never had any issues with her."

"Cool, I'll be right back."

***

The elevator dinged, and Black stepped off. With each step he took, he heard it echo through the halls. He expected it to be flooded with homicide detectives, and it was a pleasant surprise that it wasn't. After the run-in with the young boys, he wasn't in the mood for more confrontations.

He found the room he was looking for; he pushed the double doors open and stepped into the room.

"Can I help you?" The woman whom he assumed was the M.E. asked. She was taller than Black, maybe 5'7, petite, but with toned legs. She wore a business casual skirt and jacket ensemble, Navy Blue, with matching heels. Red hair pulled up into a bun, bronze tan. A little overdressed for the job, Black thought she probably had to testify in court today. He was used to seeing medical examiners in scrubs.

He walked over and extended his hand for a handshake.

"Hi, I'm Black Love, a private investigator, and you are?"

She took his hand firmly and shook it. "Deborah Kiss, what can I do for you, Mr. Love?"

"I'm working on a case and came across a name Larry Rucker. I go to see Mr. Rucker only to find out he's dead, thus the reason why I'm here."

"I don't know how long you've been a P.I., Mr. Love, but I have to tell you we don't give out information on an open investigation."

"I get it, doc, but-"

"What? Cause you're cute. I'm supposed to break the rules?"

Black smiled. "Break, Nah, I would never want you to do anything questionable."

"Because you have my best interest at heart, right?"

"Definitely. I don't have to know you not to wish you harm. Headed to court this morning?"

"Testifying in a homicide case."

"I figured it was either that or going for brunch."

She smiled. "You offering?"

"That and more, why don't you help a brother out? I promise it's for a good cause."

She tapped her foot several times, contemplating helping him, then conceded. She walked over to her laptop and tapped the keyboard until what she was looking for came across the screen.

"I can't tell you much. Two to the heart, one to the head, the first shot to the heart was the kill shot, the other two were to ensure the job."

"What else can you tell me?"

"He was on his knees."

"Can you tell me the caliber of the gun?"

"9 mil, Glock most likely."

"Any open homicides matching that caliber?"

"No, sir."

"Can I see the body?"

"Now you're pushing it."

"Pushing what?" A voice said, entering the room.

"And you are?" Deborah said as she logged off her laptop.

"Special Agent Bosselait, Major Crimes, My partner Special Agent Wu." Wu came in behind him and locked eyes with Black. "What are you doing here, Black?"

"You two know one another?" Deborah asked, eyebrow raised.

"Unfortunately, yes," Black said as he leaned against the table with his hands in his pockets.

"What can I do for you, detective?" Deborah asked as she moved around the table, positioning herself closer to Black.

"You can start by telling me how you two know one another?"

"No, you can start by letting me know if you have any official business that I can help you with?"

"You have a Larry Rucker here?"

"I do."

"That's my case."

"I see."

"A homicide case that his mother is the suspect of, well, ain't that a quinky dinky?"

"I don't know anything about that, nor do I care. As far as Mr. Rucker goes, I'll have a report for you later today."

"Wait a minute-"

She placed both hands on her hips. "Wait for what, detective?"

"I'm not done asking you two questions, like what is he doing down here?"

She looped her arm through his. "Well, not that it's any of your business. He's here to escort me to court. Then after we have brunch, as I told you before, come back later, and I'll have your report."

She walked with Black still, arm in arm, through the double doors. "Turn off the lights, will you, detective."

***

Two run-ins with Bosselait in as many days didn't sit well with Black. Finding out that he's the lead investigator in the Larry Rucker murder didn't make it any better either, and if Bosselait suspected his mother of the crime, there was a good chance that she probably did it, but why?

Life is full of conflicts, he thought, he didn't want to be complicit in murdering people, but if she had done it, she had good reason to, he thought. He didn't know for sure, all hopeful thinking by her admission she was a hired gun.

Here he was, having brunch with this woman when he should follow up on his next lead. He needed to eat, he reasoned. He also felt like this would foster another relationship for future cases, and he may need an inside man, so to speak, in the coroner's office.

She didn't bring up his mother, so he wouldn't either. She mostly went on about the case she testified in today, which was another almost two hours that he'd blown sitting through that case.

"Are you originally from Chicago?" Black asked, interrupting her dialogue about a case involving lentil soup, a fishing hook, and a rare collection of stamps.

"No, originally from Vallejo, CA."

"No shit."

"Yes sir, born and raised."

"Chicago is a long way away from home."

"Tell me about it, thank God." She let out a cantankerous laugh.

Black laughed. "Tell me how you feel about it. Why don't you?"

"No, it wasn't all bad. But another story for another day."

"Another day; planning to see me again already?"

"We'll see."

"Umm, hmm..."

"How long you been P.I.'N?"

"Not long, worked a few cases so far, think I've found my footing."

"Cool. In this case, you're working."

"What about it?"

"What's the end game? What are you trying to get out of it?"

"Clear an innocent woman's name...and keep more people from dying."

***

After dropping Deborah back off at her office, he headed towards his office. The burner phone Pepper Red gave him rang, and he hit the speaker phone button.

"Pepper Red."

"Hey, son, we need to meet at your office."

"We can't; they came by looking for you today."

"I figured they would, don't worry. I see them down the block watching."

"You see them? Where are you?"

"I'm inside already."

"What? How did you get past them?"

"I have my ways, now, come on, I don't have all night."

"I'm on my way."

Black ended the call and hit the highway, headed back towards his office; a little under thirty minutes, he was pulling onto the block. Pepper Red was right. He spotted the two plainclothes detectives watching his office. They made it so obvious a black and white guy was sitting in a parked car, and they might as well wear a uniform and sit in a patrol car. Black parked, got out, hit the alarm on his key, and entered the building.

"Pepper Red." He yelled out as he made his way through the building.

"In here, fixing a bite to eat."

He entered the kitchen to find her eating a sandwich at the counter.

"What are you doing Pepper Red? It's not safe."

"I'll be fine. I've been hiding in plain sight for decades. I know what I'm doing."

"If you say so."

"What do you got for me?"

"Not much."

"What's not much?"

"Talked to a few folks: Scat-Man, Ilene Johnson, used to be Ilene Archibald, West Side Willie's old lady."

"Yeah."

"What else you got?"

He started to tell her about the others he spoke with, the follow-up phone call with Scat-Man to meet her, and the photo but thought better of it and held it to himself.

"Some loose ends needing tying up, nothing to speak on just yet."

"I'm on a timeframe, son; the longer I stay in Chicago, the more likely I will get bagged."

"I hear you, ma. I'm on it; you are staying here tonight until they leave, right?"

She shook her head no. "Nah, I'll get past them, don't worry."

"How are you going to do that Pepper Red? Never mind, I thought this wasn't the right time or circumstances, but we haven't had much time to sit and talk about everything."

"What are you talking about? I told you everything."

"I'm not talking about the case, and you know that."

"About me leaving?"

"That doesn't matter. I'm talking about no matter how this turns out, you're still my mother, and I'm going to ride with you till the casket drops if that be the case."

"But?"

"But I'm talking about this as a second chance to get to know one another. I want to know who you are Pepper Red."

She didn't respond. Black continued. "Or am I asking for too much?"

"No, son, I-"

Someone ringing the doorbell stopped her mid-sentence, and they both became silent, locking eyes with one another. Pepper Red pulled her gun and ducked off into a nearby room. Black made his way towards the door as the bell rang each step towards the door again. He felt his feet get heavier, and his legs felt like noodles. He was surprised he made it to the door, and he thought he would pass out any second. The bell rang again. He felt lightheadedness and nausea escape him as he opened the door and stared back at him was Stone, a woman he had been seeing for a while now.

"What are you doing here, Stone?"

"Well, hello to you too." She said as she forced her way in. Black stepped to the side and closed the door.

"It's not a good time, Stone."

Pepper Red came into the room. Both women stared at one another.

"Oh, I see. Entertaining bitches, are we?"

"Stone!" Black said, grabbing one of her arms, and she yanked away.

"Don't be grabbing on me, don't be rude, introduce us."

Stone reached out her hand for a handshake. "I'm Stone, his new baby mama, and you are?"

Pepper Red folded her arms across her chest. She looked at Stone up and down from head to toe.

Stone turned and faced Black; for the first time since she entered, he paid closer attention to her appearance, and she looked pregnant. His mind shot back to the last time they were together in his office. He hadn't expected her; they had fought the day before. She continued. "Rude old bitch, ain't she? You surprise me, Black. I didn't think you were into the cougar life."

"Stone, chill. This is Pepper Red, my mother."

Stone's eyes widened; she bit her lip, turned, and faced Pepper Red.

"Congratulations." Pepper Red said as she moved past Stone.

"Give us a minute, ma."

"Umm, hmm."

***

Pepper Red didn't wait for Black to finish his discussion with Stone. She went upstairs to the top floor and went to the room at the back of the building. She opened the window and stuck one of her legs out so that she could brace herself on the sill and climb out with both feet on the sill; she barely reached the roof as she used all her strength and pulled herself up to the roof.

Once on the roof, she crawled toward the front of the building to see the street. She spotted the two detectives sitting in the car, still watching the building. Still lying on her stomach, she slowly scoots herself back to the back of the building. She stands to her feet, takes a deep breath, runs, and jumps across to the roof next door.

Not catching her breath, she ran and jumped across to the next roof, landing and running again across to the third roof. As she landed, her feet struggled to gain a good grip. The shingles on this roof were old. She felt the old shingles crumbling under her feet, making the roof slippery. She laid flat on her stomach, got an excellent grip on the ledge, and hoisted herself down, her legs dangled over a balcony. She took a breath and let go, and she fell awkwardly. Her face and chest bounced off the glass sliding door connected to the house, landing on her bottom on the balcony.

She got to her knees and crawled back to the glass door, trying to peer inside to see if she had woken anyone. When she didn't see anyone stirring, she got back to her feet, went to the balcony's railing, and climbed over, legs dangling high above the ground. She took a deep breath and let go when her feet smacked the concrete, and she felt the burn in the soles of her feet. She looked right and left down the alley, then limped a few houses down the alley, where she spotted a parked car. The headlights flashed twice. She made her way toward the car and got in.

"Thanks, Jason."

Jason was a part of Noble's network positioned in Chicago.

He laughed. "Man, Noble told me your ass was crazy."

"Just drive."

"Yes, ma'am."

***

CHAPTER NINETEEN

After seeing Stone off, Black stood on the sidewalk before his business, watching her drive off. He turned to go back up the stairs when he saw the garage light on through a window on the door. With a raised eyebrow and a smirk, Black looked back at the two detectives in the car, and they both shrugged their shoulders and laughed. He made his way to the garage and tapped on the door.

"I know you're in there, come on inside and talk, or I'll call your uncle or the cops. I haven't decided which one yet."

Black turned and headed to his office, he waved at the woman across the street, and she waived back and went inside her house. Black unlocked the door and went inside, leaving the door open.

Not long after, Johnny stepped inside, closing the door behind him.

"Hungry, kid?"

"I can eat."

"Come on," Black said as he led the way into the kitchen.

"Sit down," Black said as he went to the refrigerator, pulling mayonnaise, mustard, lunchmeat, and cheese out and setting them on the counter. He opened the breadbox on top of the fridge, removed a loaf of bread, and placed that on the counter too. "Help yourself," Black said as he placed a knife and saucer on the counter before Johnny.

Johnny stood and began making himself sandwiches. Black opened the cupboard and removed a family bag of Ruffle chips; he placed them on the counter in front of Johnny.

"Thanks," Johnny said as he ripped open the bag of chips.

Black returned to the refrigerator and removed beer and Apple juice. He set the juice on the counter in front of Johnny, popped the cap off his beer, and took a swig.

"What's going on with you, kid the truth, and no tough guy shit, just keep it real."

Johnny took a bite from his sandwich before responding. He chewed and swallowed, then answered, tears swelling in his eyes.

"I don't want to go back there."

"Back where? To your uncle?"

"Yeah, back to the life, it's not me. I wanted it to be when I was younger, but it's not in me. Uncle Mickey doesn't see it that way. He says I'm the heir to the throne. We don't get to pick what family we're born into."

"What about your mom?"

"What about her? A meth head, and who knows what else? I know, but I don't want to talk about it. It makes my stomach sick."

"Other family members? Maybe someone at school you can talk to."

"You don't get it, that's not how things are done in that neighborhood, and Uncle Mickey runs that neighborhood."

"And he's grooming you to run it someday?"

"Pretty much."

"Why not go to the cops?"

Johnny laughed. "Yeah, right. Do people around here go to the cops?"

Black smirked. "Not really."

"Exactly, Black or white poor is poor, and cops more often than not treat poor folks like shit. Besides, he's a dick, but I don't want to see him in jail. What good will that do?"

"I'm not arguing with you, kid, but why me?"

"I wasn't just in this neighborhood by chance. I came here looking for you to check you out and see what kind of guy you were."

Black finished his bottle of beer and grabbed another from the refrigerator. "And your interest in me is because of what?"

"It's in the streets, Mr. Love. You are for the kids- white, black doesn't matter, you look after kids. I saw you trending on the internet."

"That's flattering, kid, but that's a huge exaggeration."

"Is it? First, the cop's daughter, then the New Trier girls. I think I'm at the right place, and I'm right about you." Johnny reached into his pocket, removed the money that Black had given him, and placed it on the counter."

"What's that for?"

"I told you a man has to pay his just due. I want to hire you."

Black laughed. "My rates are usually slightly higher than that, but I'll bite. Hire me for what?"

"Talk with my uncle."

"And tell him what?"

"I don't know, come up with a solution to get me out of there. He won't just let me go and will need some convincing."

"I like you, kid, you're smart, but I'm not a family counselor, and albeit it's some dysfunctional street shit intertwined with it, it's still family business. Always been a rule of mine to stay out of family business, and I'm sure Mickey will see it the same."

Johnny finished the rest of his sandwich and bit into the other.

"I can respect that, and I won't beg; hell, I appreciate you just listening and for the food. One of three things for sure though you ever hear the name Johnny Sikora again. I'll be dead, in jail, or the biggest gangster this town has ever seen."

***

After getting Johnny situated for the night, he didn't have blankets or pillows. He had to go across the street to the neighbors and borrow what he needed. He made a call.

"I know it's late, Bunch, but it's important."

"Isn't it always with you, Black?"

"Need information on a guy."

"What information? What guy?"

"A Mickey Sikora and anything you got."

"Told you at the station; that was the last favor."

"I know, but if it weren't important, I wouldn't ask. It involves a kid."

"Don't throw that kid shit out at me, thinking it will pull at my heartstrings."

"Wouldn't think of it. Are you going to help me or what?"

"What about Joanne?"

"Sure, to help keep her out of trouble, I'll find something for her to do. Send her over in the morning."

"Give me a sec." Black waited; he heard clicking in the background of the call as if someone was typing on a keyboard. A few moments later, Bunchy returned. "He runs an Irish crew called themselves The Beverly Boys run the business out of a joint called Shanahan's, a bar on 30th and Union out in Bridgeport. Is this something I need to know about Love?"

"Nah, it's just a conversation."

"Need backup?"

"Got it covered; send Joanne by in the morning."

He ended the call.

***

CHAPTER TWENTY

Later that night, Black pulled onto 30th and Union, in front of Shanahan's, and parked. A car he recognized rode past, made a U-turn, and parked across the street from him, going in the opposite direction. Both men got out of their cars and met at the entrance to the bar.

Black stuck out his hand to shake Crishan's they'd met on a former case. Black helped him hide a body, literally. He owed Black a favor; Crishan was there as backup. Crishan was an inch shorter than Black, had the same weight and build, had hair cut short, skin just as dark as Black's, and had slanted eyes; he looked like an Asian/African American Hybrid. He said he was from Malaysia, from the Semang people, what people in the western hemisphere termed Negritos. Black trusted him; he knew he could hold his own.

"Thanks for coming," Black said as they embraced in a firm shake.

"Anytime, brother."

Crishan opened the door and held it open for Black. They stood at the bar, sticking out like priests in a whorehouse. Not because a Black and Asian guy walked into a primarily Irish bar but because they were strangers in a neighborhood bar.

"What can I get for you?" The bartender asked, in a less than friendly tone.

"Any cognac you got," Black said as he removed a hundred-dollar bill and placed it on the bar.

"And you?"

"A bottle of water."

"No water."

"No water?" Crishan smirked. "You serious?"

"You want water? Go to a spa."

"Give him a beer," Black said, moving the transaction along.

Mickey steps behind the bar and places his hand on the bartender's shoulder. "His money's no good here. After their drinks, they'll be leaving."

"Isn't that what everyone does? Have their drinks and leave?" Black said as he picked up his money and returned it to his pocket.

"Don't be a wise ass."

"We need to talk; your buddy here can keep my buddy company, aye?"

Mickey comes from behind the bar and goes to a booth in the back that faces the door; Black follows.

"What are you doing here, Black?"

"Oh, so you can come to my place of business unannounced, but you take issue when I do the same to you?"

"Again, Black, what do you want?"

"What do you think, Mickey? Why else would I be seen in a shithole like this?"

"The boy."

"The boy." Black held up his glass, signaling the waitress for another drink; moments later, a waitress appeared with a bottle of cognac and another glass for Mickey. She left them both on the table and was off.

"Where is he?" Mickey asked as he poured himself a drink, slid the bottle across the table to Black, and poured himself a glass.

"He's safe; he's crashing at my office."

"I want him home now; if you don't bring him, I'll send a couple of the boys to retrieve him."

"He's a smart kid that Johnny."

"Don't need you to tell me that."

"He's so smart; he knows that he's too smart to be indoctrinated into the bullshit you have in mind for him."

"Tread lightly; this is family business Black."

"I know that Mickey; that's why I'm here."

"I don't follow."

"The boy, he hired me to speak on his behalf. He wants out; he feels like being a kid; you won't value his opinion."

"Is that fucking right?"

"Fucking right paid me and everything."

Mickey laughed. "Oh, did he now? He can afford your fees, can he?"

"Client privilege I don't discuss fees and personal matters without the client's direct consent."

Mickey laughed again. Black took another swallow of the cognac and poured himself another. Mickey continued. "Look, I'm telling you once more, and I'm not telling you again; get that fucking boy back to me or-"

"Or what, Mickey?"

"You don't want to know or what."

"Nah, you don't want to know."

Mickey didn't respond; he eyed Black as he took another drink. Black continued. "He can be more than-"

"Than what, me?"

"Yes, and your brother, his mother, and everyone else that had a small moment of fame in this bullshit legacy. But ended in death, behind the wall, or a dope fiend, let the boy go."

***

CHAPTER TWENTY-ONE

B lack woke at noon, lying in bed still wearing clothes from the night before. He grabbed his phone; twelve missed calls, all from his office.

"Shit! The kid." He said, referring to Johnny; then he remembered. "The *kids*, Joanne, start work today."

He rolled out of bed, the phone still in hand, and dialed the office. Joanne answered on the first ring. He heard music in the background.

"Love Detective Agency," Joanne said in her most professional voice.

"Almost professional," Black said as he removed his shirt and pants.

"What do you mean almost?"

"The whole professional vibe is thrown off with King Von playing in the background."

"At least I got to work on time."

"Next time, kill the music before answering the phone; where's Johnny?"

"The white boy?"

"Yeah, the white boy."

"He's out front talking to the lady across the street."

"I'll be there in a minute."

He ended the call, showered, and dressed in a black Nike sweatsuit with matching Nike tennis shoes and a black White Sox baseball cap. Thirty minutes later, he was pulling up in front of his office. He tipped his hat at the officers sitting watching his office. They both gave him the finger; he laughed and went to the door. It was as Joanne had said; Johnny was with the old lady from across the street. She was talking as he was pulling the lawnmower out of the garage.

"What are you doing now? Black asked as he approached and hugged the older woman.

"I'm going to cut the nice lady's grass."

"And I'm going to pay him for his services."

"No, ma'am, my daddy taught me better than that," Johnny said as he began pushing the lawnmower across the street.

"Well, a man works; he has to get paid."

"Yes, ma'am, and I will be; it'll come back around to me in one way or another."

Black held her hand as he led her back across the street.

"Don't worry; I'll make sure he gets paid."

Black returned across the street and sat on the stairs watching Johnny mow her lawn. Not long after, Joanne stepped out and joined him.

"What's up?" Black said, not facing her.

"What's up?"

"Going be a long day."

"Yeah?"

"For me, yeah."

"What are you going to have me doing around here?" Joanne asked as she copped a squat next to him on the stairs.

"Answering phones, emails, filing cases, light cleaning around the place, you good with computer stuff?"

"What do you mean computer stuff?"

"Social media shit, I need to drum up business, you know, social media ads."

"I'll figure it out."

"Good."

"Cool." She rose from her seat and went back into the building.

***

After Johnny completed cutting the grass, Black paid him, and they both got into his car.

"I take it the talk didn't go well?"

"About as well as I expected but better than I thought."

"Not in my favor, though, right?"

"Nah, man, he said no. I'm dropping you off to him now."

"Thanks for trying."

Black didn't respond. They rode the rest of the ride in silence. Before Black could get to the block where the bar was, squad cars blocked off it. Black put the car in park and left the engine running. "Stay here."

He got out of the car and walked through the squad cars. None of the officers paid any attention to him. He forced his way to the bar just as a gurney carried out, and a white sheet covered a body. Seconds later, three men were escorted out in handcuffs. One was black, with long dreads down his back, if Black had to guess from one of the Jamaican crews from Evanston. Next was a white guy who Black assumed was from Mickey's crew, and last was Mickey. He locked eyes with Black.

"Keep an eye on him for me; I'll owe you one. You listen to him; you hear me, boy, or you'll get a hiding like never before."

Black looked behind him and saw Johnny staring back at his uncle, not responding. Black looked back at Mickey.

"Anybody, I can call for you?"

"Nah, I'm sure word has already gotten to my attorney; he'll be at the station before I arrive."

Black and Johnny watched as Mickey was loaded into the back of a squad car and driven away.

"What do I do now?"

"I don't know, kid, but we'll figure it out."

***

CHAPTER TWENTY-TWO

B lack sped into the parking space in the jam-packed hospital parking lot, cutting off a woman waiting. He hopped out of his car, slammed the door closed, and hit the alarm ignoring the woman who flashed him the finger as he dashed for the entrance. Making his way in, Black asked the receptionists for the floor to the OBGYN. After getting the information, he sprinted towards the elevator. When he stepped off the first face he saw was Stone's.

"Really, Black? I asked you to do one thing."

"Don't start. I'm here."

"You're late."

"You missed the appointment?"

"They haven't called me yet."

"Then what the hell are you talking about?"

"Scarlit Stone." The nurse called out as both Black and Stone stood and followed behind her.

"That's not the point, Black; the point is you said you were going to do something, I expect you to do it, or do you no longer keep your word?"

"Like I said, I'm here."

The nurse showed the two to the exam room. "The doctor will be with you shortly." They both nodded, and she left.

"We'll talk about this later, Black."

"No, we won't."

After sitting through the first prenatal doctor's visit, Black didn't know how to feel. He had seen things on television and thought that it would all be cliché with the hands on the belly and looking at ultrasounds and everything that came along with that, but seeing it on television and going through it was a lot more surreal. He almost felt outside of himself watching himself and Stone go through the process. Looking at her, it was as if it were her first time all over again. She looked happy. He felt a tinge of excitement; something he possibly created was growing inside her. He fought hard to hold back the smile; he didn't want to get too excited. He still had reservations about the baby being his; her ex lived with her for a while.

Stepping outside, prepared to walk her to her car and pick up where they left off with the argument, he was surprised that she hadn't brought it up.

"How do you feel, Black?"

"I don't know yet."

"That's fair. It's still new."

"Yeah."

She pressed the button on her keychain, and the doors unlocked. Black opened her car door; after she was inside, he closed the door, and she started the engine. She rolled down the window, and he leaned over and kissed her.

"Call me later," Black said as he stepped back.

"Got you. Be safe." She backed out of the parking space and pulled out as he watched her leave. He watched as Bunchy sped into the space that Stone had pulled out of; the two men nodded at one another.

"You needed to meet; I'm here," Bunchy said as he turned the engine off.

Black walked around to the passenger side of his own car and leaned into the window, grabbing the page from the photo album holding the hundred-dollar bill he had gotten from Vicki. He made his way back around to Bunchy and handed it to him. After running down his theory, Bunchy agreed to run the serial numbers and stay tight-lipped about the situation. Black told him all he knew, leaving out the parts about Pepper Red.

***

After meeting with Bunchy and getting the hundred-dollar bill to him to run the serial numbers from the bank robbery from 97, he went to see Pops. When he pulled up, Pops was sitting on the porch, Sparkle was running around the yard, and Black parked and met his father on the porch.

"How you feel, old man?"

"I'm good."

"Need some information from you."

"Shoot."

Black removed the picture and handed it to him.

Pops grunted. "Haven't seen these faces in years."

"This one here next to your mother is Larry Rucker."

"Him, I know."

"Yeah?"

"Dead."

"No shit."

Pops pointed to the next in the picture. "This here is Matt Craig. Used to run with Hambone; he was his flunkey, and Craig police now."

"What kind of police?"

"Narcotics detective."

"Who is Hambone? He in this picture?"

"No, I'm surprised those two had a love-hate relationship; as far as I hear, I never understood those two."

"You ever hear what he was into since back in the day?"

"Hambone was a wanna-be, but he was smart. He got his foot in the door through his cousin. Jessie never claimed him, but he helped him occasionally anyway. Hambone said he was one of Jessie Jackson's daddy's nephews. That's neither here nor there, but Hambone always threw the supposed family connection around. Back in the day, he made his bones as a bodyguard for one of the high-ranking members of the Black P Stone Rangers. He got out right before the war hit with the old members, the young Stones, and that whole regime change. He made enough money to put himself through school, went to the Wharton School of Business of Pennsylvania, did well for himself, and couldn't leave the streets alone. At least not at first; he's a politician now, I suppose still crooked, maybe but out the streets."

"A politician?"

"Yeah, son Hambone an Alderman now."

"Alderman Berber?"

"Yes, sir."

"I got word he was looking for Pepper Red too and asking about me; you know why?"

Pops shook his head no. "Be careful, son; political gangsters play by different rules."

"I got this, Pops; I'm not playing their game, and Berber is no gangster."

***

CHAPTER TWENTY-THREE

S itting at his desk, cognac in front of him, Black examined the picture of his mother. He would need to confront her about it; he needed hard proof first; otherwise, she would deny it. Telling him about past bodies was one thing, but a stash of twenty million dollars was another son or no son; he didn't see her coming up off that information willingly. He stared at his mother; she was so young. He moved from face to face; he looked at the building in the photo, and there were words on the building that he couldn't make out. He laughed.

"I will have to invest in an old-school magnifying lens."

He snapped a picture of the photo with his phone and emailed it to himself. He opened his laptop and retrieved the email. Black blew the screen up. The words on the front of the building read Big Heart Commercial Development. He snapped another, focusing on one of the men in the picture at the end. He zoomed in on the man in the picture. What looked like it could be a woman's arm hung around the man's neck. The unidentified woman was cut out of the photo; the person who took the picture only captured her arm. Black zoomed in on the woman's arm, and a tattoo was on the inside of her wrist—a figure eight.

"Mr. Love!"

"Yeah," Black said. She startled him; it was Joanne; he had no idea how long she had been knocking he was lost in thought.

"It's my dad; he's on line one."

Black picked up the phone sitting on his desk and pressed line one.

"What's this I hear about you harboring a known fugitive?"

"That's bullshit, Bunchy, and you know it."

"Do I?"

Black thought to question Bunchy about how he knew about his mother but decided not to; he knew cops could sometimes be gossipy. He learned that from his time as D.A.; besides, he had no idea how much he knew and didn't know.

"Joanne isn't in danger if you're worried about that."

"That's not what I hear."

"What do you want me to do? Send her home?"

"You can tell my father I'm not quitting, Mr. Love, he wanted to get me a job where I didn't quit after a week, and this is it. I like it here."

Black looked up, annoyed. "Don't listen to my phone calls; go do something."

She rolled her eyes and went back downstairs.

"You hear that?"

"I heard it."

"It's your call; she's your daughter."

Bunchy sighed. "She's eighteen and thinks she knows every damn thing. Is she safe, yes, or no?"

"Definitely."

"I'm trusting you Love, don't let me regret it."

Black ended the call."

***

Disappointed about the call from Bunchy, he understood the concerns he may have had about his daughter's safety. Still, he hoped it was information about the hundred-dollar bill and whether the serial number matched. Black returned downstairs, entering through the kitchen, and both Johnny and Joanne were down there. Black stood at the bottom of the stairs, watching. The teens paid no attention to him. Joanne had her face in her phone, a hot pocket on a plate in front of her. Johnny, with wings and fries in front of him on a plate, and Johnny's eyes locked on Joanne. She was at least three years older than him, her being eighteen. It was obvious the boy had a crush on her. Black smirked. Johnny was out of his depth with the young woman.

"What are you two doing?"

Joanne didn't respond; she kept scrolling through her phone. Johnny looked up, startled.

"Nothing much."

The doorbell rang, and Black reached the door, leaving the two teens alone.

"Who is it?" Black yelled through the door.

"Conner, I'm here about Johnny; Mickey sent me."

Black opened the door. Standing on the other side of the door was an average-height, medium-sized guy with blonde hair and a t-shirt covered with a leather jacket, jeans, and boots. He held a midsized leather satchel.

"What can I do for you?" Black asked, still guarding the door, leaving Conner outside.

"Like I said, Mickey sent some stuff for the kid."

Black hesitated for a second, then let him in; he closed the door behind his guest. Johnny and Joanne had joined the men by this time, neither speaking.

Conner unzipped the bag and handed Black a manila envelope.

"What's this?" Black asked as he opened the sealed envelope.

"Mickey's lawyer sent it and said something about giving you temporary legal guardianship of the kid. You have the discretion of where he goes to school, where he lives, and other stuff outlined in that envelope."

"Wait a minute, shouldn't I be talking to a lawyer?"

"You are a lawyer, ain't you?"

"Yeah, but not a family lawyer."

"Look, man, don't give me a hard time; I'm just the messenger; he said to sign the papers and give em to me; everything is legal."

He opened the bag wider to show Black what was inside it.

"Mick sent money to feed the kid, clothes, or anything else he might need."

"Hold on, how long is he asking me to keep the kid for?"

"Not sure; his lawyer is on it. Mick, don't get me wrong, I love the guy, but if his case looks good or not, he ain't going tell me what's going on; it'll be a wait-and-see situation."

He turned and faced Johnny. "And you, Mickey, told me to check in on you occasionally. You don't go to school; you don't get passing marks; you get into trouble at school; you give Mr. Love any trouble here. He permitted me to discipline you the way I see fit. And how do I see fit?"

"With me having a busted lip and black eye."

He placed his hands in his pockets. "As long as we have an understanding." He turned his back to Johnny and addressed Black again. "You signing them papers or what? I have other business."

"I have to have someone look over them, and I'll get em back to you at the bar, alright?"

"That's fine, don't take too long; Mickey was clear on that; he said to tell you that he paid a lot of money and pulled some strings to keep this out of family court, but that will only last for so long, he's the kid's only living relative worth a damn so social services will come and snatch the kid out of here."

"I hear you, but the money."

"What about it?"

"Can't take it."

Conner stepped around Black making his way back to the door. "Spend it on the kid, burn it, give it away. I was told to get it to you; I got it to you; what you do with it is your business."

He opened the door and stepped out; Black stood with the door open, watching as he got into the passenger seat of an idling Camaro. Black stepped back inside and closed the door before the car pulled off.

***

CHAPTER TWENTY-FOUR

A giant of a man, aging yet sturdy 6'11, equally bulky as he is tall, looks like a retired athlete, looks as if he could've played defensive tackle for the Chicago Bears. Big Willie, William, or those who knew his reputation, called him Big Heart. He walked down Chicago's West Side K-Town streets with his lieutenant Ray-Ray. Big Heart shook his head, sadly looking at what had become of his old neighborhood.

"How did you let it come to this?" Big Heart pointed at abandoned houses, burned down houses, and vacant lots where homes used to be. They stopped in front of one of the few remaining buildings on the block. A duplex, the bottom apartment had a glowing fluorescent sign in the window that read "Big Heart Commercial Development."

"This was a long time in the making, boss; the city stopped pumping money into the community's infrastructure, unorganized gangs with no damn sense shooting up everything. It's like the Wild West out here since you've been gone. Most of the cats that held it down were dead, in jail, or on dope. Nobody respects nothing."

"It breaks my heart."

"We barely held on to this place, boss; some white folks came in trying to buy us out, some big downtown firm hell half these shit holes you see on this block they own, I'm sure they're going to fix em up and gentrify white folks going start moving in by the boatload."

"And I'm going be the last holdout; they want this neighborhood nigger free. They are going to have to pay me handsomely."

Ray-Ray pulls a Pall Mall cigarette from his pants pocket, places it between his lips, lights it, takes a long hard pull, and blows out the smoke before continuing.

"They sure as hell got the money."

"What are we doing around here for muscle?"

"We have a few new faces, but getting fresh blood is hard. Everyone wants to be boss until they catch a R.I.C.O. charge for dumb shit, a funky-ass kilo or two, or a half-ass dope house trying to live out their Tony Montana dreams. I blame the rap music. Fucking YouTube and got damn TikTok."

"What the hell are you jabbering about?"

"You'll learn soon enough."

"Who's the best hitter we got?"

"A young boy named Blake, off of Kilbourn."

"Yeah, we know any of his people?

"Yeah, he is one of the Norfleet's."

"Related to the Norfleets that ran those little sections off of Lavergne and Lawler?"

"The nephew."

"Whatever happened to them?"

"The older brother has been dead, heard, baby bro in the Feds, Pennsylvania, I heard."

"You say the boy thorough?"

"A little green, but not as wild as the others."

"Get him in my office."

Ray-Ray nodded in agreement. "Pepper Red?"

Big Heart didn't respond. He walked up the stairs and into his office.

***

CHAPTER TWENTY-FIVE

B lack was on the highway headed towards K-Town to the building address he found online. It wasn't hard to put two and two together and find the place. Pepper Red had told him about Lil G-Man's uncle Big Heart, and the words on the side of the building in the picture read Big Heart Commercial Development. He Googled the business name for an address, and nothing came up. Next, he keyed in Big Heart Commercial Development on the Duns & Bradstreet website. A website that tracks business entities and stores their business credit scores.

The listed owners were William Mossberry and Gerald Eggleston. Black made his way up the stairs and tapped on the door on the first floor. He twisted the doorknob and walked in before anyone could answer. Black was surprised to find that the space had been modernized. Judging from the outside of the building, he expected outdated furniture, old carpeting, and peeling wallpaper or paint.

The waiting area had white marble flooring, leather and steel furniture, and modern abstract paintings covering the walls. Jazz from Albert Collins played throughout the establishment. To the right of the waiting area was a set of double glass doors; the doors opened, and a young man, who looked to be early twenties, stepped out. He wore jeans, Jordans, and a Chicago Bulls tee, and his hair was in locks with a fresh lineup.

"What can I do for you?" The young man asked, keeping Black back at arm's length.

"I'm here to see William Mossberry."

"Who's looking for him?"

"Tell him it's Black Love, a Private Investigator."

"Wait here."

The young man left the door slightly ajar and went back inside. A few seconds later, he returned and led Black into the room. When Black stepped into the room, he saw that it was an office. The young man closed the door behind them and stood before it. Big Heart sat behind his big oak desk; it looked vintage, no doubt had been there since the 70s or 80s. Two overstuffed leather chairs sat in front of the desk. Across from the desk was a loveseat; a man in his late sixties was sitting there smoking a cigarette wearing a Fedora and gray three-piece suit and tie, with matching alligator shoes.

"Pepper Red's boy?" Big Heart asked, opening a wooden box on his desk and removing a cigar. Black nodded. He continued. "This should be interesting."

Black stepped up to his desk and placed his hands on the back of the leather chair. "I'm here to ask you some questions, Mr. Mossberry...alone."

"You can speak in front of them; this is Ray-Ray, been with me for over thirty-five years, and the young lion behind you is my protégé in training Blake. Speak your mind."

"It's about the First National Bank."

Big Heart raised an eyebrow, placed the cigar in his mouth, bit off the tip, and spit the tip in a trash can sitting near his desk. He didn't respond; Black continued.

"I know you were a part of the heist of 97 for twenty million dollars."

Big Heart still didn't respond. He lit the cigar, took a few puffs, and blew the smoke out. Black continued.

"I also know that you blamed my mother for the hit on Lil G-Man; I'm here to tell you that she didn't do it."

"Tell me this, since you know about a supposed hit on a bank, and you know for a certainty your mother didn't kill my nephew, you seem to know a lot about my business; why don't you tell me this Black Love Private Investigator, tell me where Pepper Red is."

"I couldn't say."

Big Heart and Ray-Ray both laughed.

"Of course, you can't."

Black removed the picture and placed it on Big Heart's desk. Big Heart picked it up, smiled, and returned it to his desk.

"And this proves what?"

Black picked up the picture and placed it back into his pocket. Big Heart continued. "That's what I thought; you don't know Jack shit, boy. You going have to get a more convincing poker face before you come in here trying to bluff me, son."

"No, bluff."

"No proof." Big Heart continued. "You get one warning; next time I see you, you best have your mother with you; we have some things we need to clear up."

Blake grabbed Black's arm; Black yanked away, pushed him back, and pulled his gun, had it aimed at Blake. He nodded towards the desk. "Over there, hands on the desk," Black ordered as Blake did as he was instructed.

"You're not stopping anything; the bounty is still active." Big Heart said, leaning back in his seat.

"Cancel it," Black demanded, gun still pointed at Blake.

"Wouldn't matter; it's in a black-market escrow account; when proof of death is validated, the funds are released."

Black pointed the gun at Blake's right hand, planted it firmly on the desk, and pulled the trigger. He crumpled to his knees, squealing.

"For your sake, you better hope no one collects that bounty, or I'll be back, and next time it won't be a hand; I put a hole in."

Black backed out of the room and out of the building.

***

CHAPTER TWENTY-SIX

Pepper Red drove through Maywood thinking. She was becoming impatient with Black's progress. He called with bad news and wanted to meet at the office. Lost in thought, she hadn't noticed that the light had changed and cruised through the red light. When she realized what she had done, it was too late. She looked into her rearview mirror to see if any police were behind her. Luckily for her, there were none, but she noticed another car blowing through the light behind her. She was being followed by who she didn't know-Big Heart's people? The police, maybe? She slowed her pace to see if the car following would also; when they had, she sped up, running through another red light. She saw a flash but ignored it and continued driving. She looked into her mirror again, just as the first time the car also took that red light.

Pepper Red ran another red light and saw the flash again. It dawned on her that the traffic light had taken her photo, and the car was behind her again. Pepper Red slowed down and made a U-turn, going back in the direction she had come from; she drove past the car following her. She stole a glance and got the make and model of the vehicle, and she also got a glimpse of the person following her; it was a woman. Pepper Red removed her gun and sat it on her lap, looking at the car in the rearview mirror to see if she would follow; when she hadn't Pepper Red sped up and headed to see Black.

***

Five miles from Black's office, a black and white police patrol car with an officer sitting behind the wheel, getting ready to end his shift for the night, nods at a couple pulling up next to him on a crotch rocket. They both wore tinted helmets covering their faces. The bike stops, and the woman gets off; she removes a gun and starts firing at the officer, he takes several shots to the chest before the woman hops back onto the bike and it takes off. The officer makes it to his car radio and calls in the shooting.

***

The two detectives, apart of Bosselait's team, are still sitting and watching Black's office.

"Tell me again why we don't call this in?" Detective Lumpkin, the Black cop, the younger of the two, asks; he's only been with the unit a few months, handpicked by Bosselait and Wu transferred in from Narcotics.

Hendrix, the senior of the two, was an old-timer, a part of a long line of old Irish cops. Lumpkin always wondered how he got the name, Hendrix. He didn't know much about him other than he used to work in Internal Affairs and was on the verge of being fired until Bosselait swooped in and made him a part of his unit.

"Bosselait told us about the kid and his uncle, we'll put it in our notes in case it connects in some way down the line, but right now, our objective is this Mohammed chick."

"We have a 999 on the corner of 116th and Halsted!" The call blared through the radio attached to Lumpkins' hip. He removed the radio and spoke into it.

"Plainclothes officers Lumpkins and Hendrix en route."

"Son of a bitch!" Hendrix said as he turned the car on and sped from the block. A few moments later, a car pulled up in front of Black's office. Pepper Red got out and went inside.

***

Black sat in the waiting area of his office, having a more potent drink than beer D'usse VSOP Cognac, his drink of choice, sat before him Pepper Red walked in.

He laughed. "I see why Pops was in love with you."

"What are you talking about?" she asked as she took the glass he was drinking from his hand and drank the rest.

"Pour me another."

Black took the glass from her and poured another drink. "How did you get past the detectives outside Pepper Red?"

"A woman has her secrets; didn't Pope teach you that?"

He frowned and handed her the glass. He picked up another glass and poured himself a shot. She laughed.

"Don't pout, oh God, you are your father's son. I had some people I know roll up on an officer and create a 999."

"A 999? You had someone shoot the police?"

She shrugged. They didn't use actual bullets; it was a pellet gun and looked and sounded real enough. If he wore a vest, he'll be fine, just a little shaken up; if he didn't, he'd have some welts on his chest. No blood, no loss of life, no must, no fuss. But everyone knows if there is a code 999 officer down, all police within a 20-mile radius will drop everything and respond."

"Including those on a stake out."

"Exactly, so I say we have maybe an hour before I go."

"And they won't trace it back to you?"

"I only work with professionals, now this Bosselait cop you told me about, if he's any good, he'll figure it out, but he won't have any proof. So, it's safe to say we can only use this trick once."

"Well, just a little FYI, we have company upstairs."

"Who, ya baby mama?"

"Not funny, Pepper Red."

"I ain't laughing, and I ain't get her pregnant don't get shitty with me."

"No, it's not her; it's Johnny. The white kid from before."

"What is the deal with him?"

"Long story, but not him, another kid I hired as a secretary."

"What are you running a daycare? Can they be trusted?"

"Can anybody?"

"That doesn't make me feel any more assured, son."

"It'll be fine; this will all be sorted out before you know it."

There was a knock at the door, then it opened. They both paused as they watched Trigger walk in. She and Pepper Red locked eyes. Black introduced the t wo.

"Pepper Red, this is Trigger Brown, Trigger Pepper Red, my mother."

Pepper Red took her hand into a handshake.

"Nice to meet you." Trigger said as the two women stared one another down.

"Look at her; I see you have your father's taste."

"What are you talking about, ma?"

"You don't see it?"

"See what?'

"You and she are Pope and I, thirty years ago."

Black laughed. "We're not opening that can of worms Pepper Red; this is not a family therapy session we're going to have."

"Here he goes, being over dramatic." Trigger said as she took the glass of Cognac from his hand and downed it in one swallow. Black shook his head as he went into the kitchen to retrieve another glass.

"As I said, your father's son."

"He's probably feeling embarrassed that he does have the same taste as Pops in women, and that scares him."

"Scares him? Why?"

"Some psychologists say boys who grow to be men and date or marry the type of women their fathers were attracted to or women their fathers married. Or, more specifically, said boy's mother, according to these psychologists, these boys have a deep-rooted desire to fuck their mothers."

"Oh God, if that ain't some white folks mess there."

"Again, not talking about it Pepper Red. What are you doing here, Trigger?" Black said as he re-entered the room and re-filled their glasses and his as well."

"Full disclosure, I came to meet Pepper Red, woman to woman."

"Now that your covers' blown, right?"

Trigger smiled sheepishly.

"What are you two talking about?" Black asked as his eyes moved from woman to woman, waiting for a response.

"Don't play stupid, son. I know you put her on me."

"Put her on you? Again what are you talking about?"

"You had your girlfriend here following me."

"I'm not his girlfriend; I'm nobody's girl, and I haven't been a girl for a long time." She downed her drink and held the empty glass up for Black to re-fill while never breaking eye contact with Pepper Red.

"The old man." Pepper Red said as she downed her drink and held it up for Black to re-fill.

Black filled both glasses. "Pops, why?"

"Overprotective." Pepper Red said as she moved towards the waiting area to sit. Trigger followed her lead and sat in a chair across from her.

"Pops asked me to have your back, said if you knew, you would object and not cooperate."

"That does not sound like Pope; what did he say?"

"You were a stubborn brat, and would ditch me the first chance you got, so he didn't want you to know."

"Now that sounds like Pops," Black said as he finally was able to take a swallow of the Cognac.

"I figured since you made me, I might as well come clean; no need in having you more worried than you need to be."

"I appreciate it. I like this one, Black."

"This one? How many has she met, Black?"

Black stood. "Let me go check on our guest upstairs."

Trigger winked at Pepper Red and smiled. As Black went to get another liquor bottle, he returned, and the ladies were laughing and talking amongst themselves.

"Scat-Man wants to meet."

"Fuck Scat-Man."

"I thought he was your right hand back in the day."

"That was back in the day. He didn't want to help when you first reached out, and now suddenly, he's changed his heart. I have the right mind to-"

Black cut her off mid-sentence.

"Big Heart wants to meet too," Black said as he sat across from them.

Pepper Red smirked. "Well, ain't I popular? He'll fuck around and meet his maker; we cross paths, and he doesn't tell me what I want to hear."

"And that be what Pepper Red, I thought this was about clearing your name?"

She downed her drink before responding. "It is."

"Don't seem like it."

"I don't care what it seems like, son. I'm telling you what it is."

"If you say so."

"Just say that shit Black; get it off your chest."

Trigger stood. "Maybe I should go."

Pepper Red waived her comment off. "Child relax; we're just talking."

"Yeah, Trigger, this is our mother/son moment."

Pepper Red laughed. "Is that what this is? Go ahead, get it all out; tell me how terrible of a mother I am and how I ruined your life."

This time Black laughed. "No, you can ease your conscious on that one, Pepper Red; you didn't ruin my life. You didn't improve my life. You added nothing to it, good or bad, and I'm a better man for it." He grabbed Trigger by the arm and pulled her to her feet, and she fell into his arms. He spoke into her ear. "Get your shit. I'm about to take you home and fuck the shit out of you."

She cleared her throat. Pulled from Black's grasp, she rolled her eyes. She turned and picked up her purse.

"It was nice meeting you, Pepper Red; I'll be out in the car; Black, don't be long."

After she was gone, Black handed the bottle to Pepper Red. I will sleep on it, and you'll sleep on it. Let me know in the morning who you want to meet with Scat-Man or Big Heart."

Pepper Red nodded. He turned and walked out.

***

CHAPTER TWENTY-SEVEN

E arly the following day, after dropping Trigger back off to her car, she left it parked in front of his office. He was surprised to find the detectives still hadn't returned. After Trigger was in her car and driving off, he was to meet Pepper Red at Scat-Man's place, and she had already gone ahead of him. Before he left the block, he heard the sirens behind him and looked into the rearview mirror; it was a black Expedition truck with flashing lights. He pulled to the side of the road and turned the engine off. He looked in his mirror as Bosselait approached; he held a manila folder in his hand and tapped on his window.

"We need to talk."

Black got out of the car and leaned against it. "What's up?"

Bosselait opened the folder and removed the banknote Black had given Bunchy, which was sealed in an evidence bag. He held it up so that Black could see it. "We got a hit for that serial number you wanted to be looked into."

Black didn't respond. Bosselait folded his arms across his chest and continued. What are you doing with an old note from an unsolved bank robbery?"

Black still didn't respond. He chewed the inside of his jaw, silently stewing; Bunchy had turned on him. Seeing Black was unlikely to respond, Bosselait pressed more.

"This wouldn't have anything to do with your fugitive mother, would it? I think we had this all wrong about your moms; maybe she was in on the heist and killed Lil G Man for the money."

"You're fishing, Bosselait."

He placed the hundred-dollar bill back into the envelope and removed a grainy picture from a traffic camera. In the picture was what looked like a Black woman. I couldn't make her out 100%, but as well as Bosselait could tell, Black could too. It was a good chance that it was Pepper Red in that photo.

"Who's that?" Black asked, sounding disinterested.

"Don't fucking play with me, Love."

"Don't fucking waste my time Bosselait. Is there something you want or not? I have someplace to be."

"Yeah, where's that?"

"I'm going to get some pussy; where the fuck are you going?"

Bosselait smirked. "Yeah, I bet you are; get out of here."

"Fuck you very much, officer."

Bosselait returned to his vehicle, got in, and made a U-turn; they drove off in opposite directions.

***

CHAPTER TWENTY-EIGHT

The door was slightly ajar when Black arrived at Scat-Man's place. He nudged the door open, stuck his head inside, and looked around; he found the place eerily silent. He pulled his gun and tip-toed as he made his way to the living room, only to find Scat-Man on the floor stinking up the room with Pepper Red standing over him, holding her gun as well.

"Got damn Pepper Red."

"I didn't do it."

"You didn't do it?"

"He can't do nothing for me dead."

Black didn't respond. She continued. "We got to go."

"You see anything around here that might be a clue to lead me to who did this?"

"Wasn't looking for none; you're the detective, not me."

Black looked around the room for anything out of place, and he noticed the half-eaten sandwich on the floor near Scat-Man's body. Pepper Red walked towards the exit as Black entered the kitchen to find something to wrap the sandwich in. He returned shortly after rummaging through the kitchen cabinets with two zip-lock sandwich bags. Black used one of the bags to pick up the sandwich and the other to seal the sandwich in. Before leaving, he grabbed another sandwich bag and Scat-Man's toothbrush from the bathroom to match his DNA for testing against the sandwich. After making it outside, Black looked up and down the block to find Pepper Red was gone. He dialed her number she sent him to voice mail.

***

CHAPTER TWENTY-NINE

Black pulled into the parking lot of Travis & Travis Accounting in River Forest, IL. He got out of the car and walked into the building. He stood by the door and surveyed the place. It was a storefront building and no receptionist. A vending machine filled with snacks to the right. Beyond that, two desks sit side by side, across from those desks, and another two sit side by side. Black continued towards the center of the room. Greeting him were a bronzed man and woman team, both similar in height, looked to be former athletes, both tall and toned.

"Hello, my name is Black Love. I'm a private detective and spoke with someone on the phone about a case I'm working on."

The man extended his hand for a handshake. "Nice to meet you, Mr. Love. I'm Randolph, and this is my wife, Alicia."

She nodded at Black, and he nodded back and followed the pair back to another set of desks that faced one another; the two desks kissed in the back of the building.

***

After meeting with the Travis's, he was back on the highway, and an hour later, he was at his destination. Huntley, IL, felt like he was in the middle of nowhere. He pulled into the parking space in front of the facility for the mentally disturbed parked. Before getting out, Black looked over the little information he could find on the internet about Alderman Berber, the Alderman was asking people about him. Black thought it was only fitting to return the favor and dig into his life a little bit. Besides, he needed to get ahead of this thing. Everywhere he turned, bodies were turning up. He exited the car, walked into the building, and asked to see Tamara Berber. It wasn't long before he was escorted to a waiting area and sat; she was brought to him not long after. She didn't speak; she smiled and sat. After the nurse was gone, she looked into Black's eyes; her eyes iced over, and gone was her meek demeanor. After some internet searching, Black learned of an old court case that made the news about Alderman Berber and his wife, which led him to the Huntley Facility.

"Who the hell are you?"

"Black Love, a private investigator, I must ask you some questions."

"Questions about what?"

"Your husband, among other things."

"Why don't you ask him?"

"Because I'm asking you."

"What I get out of helping you?"

"What do you want?"

"I want to get out of here."

"I can't help you with that."

She stood to leave; he grabbed her hand. "Wait."

She yanked her hand away. "Wait for what?"

"I'll get you out."

"You just said you couldn't."

"Ma'am. I'll get you out."

She stared back and crossed her arms across her chest. "Why should I believe you?"

"Because I said I would."

"Not enough. If you're here asking questions about my husband, you know how powerful he is; how do I know you have what it takes to get the job done?"

"I got in to see you, didn't I?"

She unfolded her arms, let her shoulders relax, and slumped into the chair across from him. "What do you want to know about Lerone?"

"What does he have to do with a woman named Sharon Miner Mohamed?"

She laughed. "That's a name I haven't heard in a thousand years. Nothing that I know of, what she to you?"

"She's my mother."

"Really? You Pepper Red's boy."

"Are you sure about Berber and my mother?"

She shrugged. "If there was anything between those two, it's new to me. Were they messing around or something?"

Black shook his head no. "Not that I know of."

"What's this all about, young man?"

"I need information, the information I think you have, and I need it fast, or a lot of people are going to get hurt."

"I don't know what to tell you."

"Start with Larry Rucker, used to go by-"

"Westside Willie, why on God's green Earth are you bringing up these folks I ain't thought or cared about since forever?"

"What do you know about him?"

"Again, nothing, shit he hustles, I guess, or dead, in prison, maybe shit, I don't know. He was a ladies' man, not my type, but I could see why the ladies would go for him. If he had business with Lerone, Lerone never shared it with me."

"Well, you got one of the three right; Westside Willie is dead. Killed a few days ago."

She shrugged. "Well, good for him."

"Ma'am?"

"Didn't expect him to live as long as he had; good he lived to be that old. What are you going to do to get me out of here?"

"One more name, ma'am; what about Gerald Eggleston?"

She stared into the distance; she fought back a smile, then her eyes watered.

"Ma'am?" he asked again.

"Yes, I knew Gerald. I knew Gerald very well."

Black remained silent. She wiped tears from her eyes with the back of her hand. Black zoned in on the tattoo of figure eight on the inside of her wrist.

He reached into his pocket, removed a handkerchief, and handed it to her. She wiped her eyes dry and handed it back. He placed it back into his pocket.

"What do you want to know about him?" She asked, more composed.

"Were you two having an affair?"

She turned her head to meet his eyes. "It felt more like I was having an affair with Lerone on Gerald."

"And you knew about him and my mother?"

She smiled. "Child, I knew about Gerald and all the other women, and he just had this way about him. I can't explain it, it was accept him in his world or not have him in yours, so I accepted it."

"Why not just leave your husband?"

"Lerone was sweet...in the beginning. He was a provider. He wasn't a strong man, but I knew he would always care for me; what woman doesn't want to be taken care of?"

"You mind if I ask, why are you in here? You seem of sound mind and body when we've been talking."

"I'm in here because I loved Gerald."

"Excuse me?"

"Lerone found out, said he loved me too much to kill me or let another man have me, so he hired some slick talking lawyer put some psychologists in his pockets to lie to the courts say I was out my mind and a danger to myself been in here for years now."

"What about relatives?"

"Family never had much money; they go along to get along; he pays their bills, and they act like this place and me being here is best for me."

"One last question, you think your husband killed Gerald?"

"Lerone?" She laughed. "That coward, God no. But did he pay to have it done? I think so. Can I prove it? No. And the thing that hurts the most is not to be cold-hearted but to tell the truth. I could have accepted that if Lerone had killed Gerald because he loved me and I was his woman. I could have respected that. The fact he had Gerald killed not from wounded honor. Or another man was bedding his wife. It was over a bruised ego. It was vindictive and mean. He had Gerald killed because he knew me losing him would break my heart."

"What do you know about the First National heist?"

"The what?"

"The bank robbery of 97 for twenty million dollars."

"Am I supposed to know something about it?"

"You admitted that you and Lil G-Man were having an affair; he would've told you."

"So was Pepper Red? Did you grill her like you're grilling me?"

Black's jaw tightened. "Did you know anything or not, lady?"

"Say, wallah." An Islamic phrase, the context slightly altered for the youth essentially meant *are you serious?* She continued. "What? Will you slap me around if I don't answer?"

Black was familiar with the phrase *say wallah* it struck a familiar chord. "What? No, what are you talking about?"

She chuckled. "Relax, I'm just fucking with you. Men didn't talk to women about their business in those days. If anyone knows anything, it would've been his uncle Big Heart; that's who I would talk to."

Black removed his phone from his pocket and dialed a number.

"What are you doing?"

"Calling in some favors, going to get you out of here...hello, Veronica, I need a favor, it'll mean bringing down an Alderman, and you don't have to do much heavy lifting.... For starters, I had forensic accountants looking into these old players' business holdings, William Mossberry, and Gerald Eggleston. The emails are still coming in as they uncover more information, but they've found shell cooperations linked to Gerald Eggleston. He has a property in Fernwood Park called Twin Infinity Real Estate. They haven't reported any income since his death. But the property taxes on the property have been paid every year right on time since his passing. I know it's a long shot, but I got a plan."

Black listened for a few seconds, then ended the call.

"Take down an Alderman? You're going after Lerone?"

"Is that a problem?"

"Not if it will help get me out of here."

***

CHAPTER THIRTY

After the meeting with Tamara Berber, Black had more questions than answers. Speeding down the highway, he dialed Bunchy; Bunchy answered at the first ring.

"What's up, Black?"

"I need you to go to evidence lock up and sign out the evidence on the Eggleston murder."

"The what?"

"Eggleston happened back in the '90s, first name Gerald."

"Not my case, Love; you know I'm not homicide, right."

"I got a hunch. Bring the detective whose case it is with you if you have to. Just get that evidence to the Cook County Medical examiner's office. You owe me, Bunchy."

Black ended the call before he could oppose. One hour later, he was pulling into the parking lot and entering the building. Black phoned ahead to M.E. Kiss, and she met him in the lobby. When they stepped into the morgue, Bunchy was there waiting and handed the evidence bag to the doctor.

"First, the hundred-dollar bill with the serial numbers, now this, you have me involved in a lot of moving parts and giving me nothing to go on; you want to tell me what this is all about, Love?"

Kiss set the bag on the table and slid on a pair of latex gloves.

"I'd like to know that as well." She said as she ripped open the plastic evidence bag.

Black reached into the bag he was carrying and removed the handkerchief Tamara gave him to wipe her eyes with and the half-eaten sandwich and toothbrush he got from Scat-Man's place. He placed it on the table next to the contents of the evidence bag.

"Run a sample from the handkerchief against the blood from these clothes from the victim. Also, run DNA tests on these things here as well."

Without any protest, Kiss went to work. Black and Bunchy stepped to the side and spoke in whispers.

"Where are you going with this man?"

"If I'm correct, this will blow this case wide open, solve a twenty-plus-year-old cold case, and exonerate my mother."

"Other things I'd like to discuss."

"You mean you ratting me out to Bosselait?"

"It wasn't like that. I didn't reach out to Bosselait word got out; I was looking into the banknote, and he came to me, besides the badge comes first always."

"I'll keep that in mind going forward."

"Do that. What's this I hear about you keeping the boy of that white thug arrested for murder around my daughter?"

"Bosselait told you that too?"

"As a matter of fact, he did."

"Wait a minute, hold on, where the hell do you get off questioning me about my business?"

"When that business affect my daughter?"

"Am I going to have to separate you two?" Kiss asks, still working on the task at hand.

Neither of the men responds. They step a few feet further away and continue the conversation. Bunchy pulled out a chair and sat, removed a deck of cards, opened the box, and began shuffling.

"You don't want her to work there; that's your call, but don't think you're about to run shit up in my spot."

"Cop a squat, Love."

"What are you talking about?"

Bunchy began dealing the cards. "We'll be here at least 90 minutes waiting on these results."

Black didn't argue and pulled out a chair and joined him at the table. The two played tonk, ceasing with the back and forth about Joanne, Johnny, and the gangsters. Almost two hours had passed.

"I got a hit," Kiss said, looking at the results.

Black and Bunchy made their way over to the doctor.

"What we got, doc?" Black asked, peering over her shoulder.

"We got a couple of things going here."

"I'm listening."

"Okay, so the first thing, the fluids found on the victim match the handkerchief."

"Who's is it, Love?" Bunchy asked, joining in the conversation.

"It's mine, and I let Tamara Berber use it."

"Berber? Why does that name sound familiar?"

"Tamara Berber is the wife to the Alderman."

"No shit."

"Interesting," Kiss said with a mischievous smile.

"How so?" Black asked, interests piqued.

Kiss picked up the file of the original M.E.'s report and ran her finger across the file until she found what she was looking for.

"The sample from this handkerchief matches a sample of saliva taken from the murder victim's genitals."

Bunchy laughed. "So, he was banging Alderman Berber's wife? The husband, it's always the husband." Bunchy said as if he had solved the crime himself.

Black shook his head no. "I don't like him for this."

"And why the hell not?"

"There's more to it." Black spread the contents of the police report across the table, looking at the photos from the original autopsy. He focused on the tattoo on little G-Man's chest. There it was again, a tattoo of the infinity symbol. It reminded him of something Scat-Man said: *(he got his broads branded)*. Black kept the thought to himself.

"More to it or not, I'm passing this on to the lead detective on this case."

"You said there were a few things?" Black asked, directed towards Kiss.

She slid the sandwich he'd brought in, now sealed, into a plastic evidence bag. She also slid over the results from the separate short tandem repeat tests, the name of the test used to identify DNA. She also slid over another evidence bag; a small silver metallic object was inside. Black picked up the bag and looked at it.

"What is it?"

"It is an Amalgam Bonding."

"A what?" Bunchy asked, leaning in towards Black to get a closer look.

"It's a silver filling," Black said, answering her. "Who does it belong to?" Black asked, directed towards Kiss.

"Your guess is as good as mine, it didn't match any fluids found on the victim, and it's not in the system. We only know that whoever ate this sandwich is missing a filling, found it wedge in there."

"He didn't feel it come out?" Bunchy asked.

"Probably not; I would imagine he was in so much pain from neglecting to go the dentist when it did come out. It just felt like his normal level of pain."

'What about the other things I brought in?" Black asked, moving the conversation along.

"They didn't match any of the other samples you brought in."

That meant Black could rule out Scat-Man as Lil G Man's killer. He would keep that information to himself, and he didn't need them asking questions he didn't want to answer; he would have to tell them about finding Scat-Man's body. "Cool."

"You want to tell me what this means, Love?" Bunchy asks now, becoming agitated.

"It means I'm still missing some pieces," Black said as he headed towards the door. "I'll call you later, doc," Black said as he headed towards the exit.

"We're not done talking about this, Love," Bunchy said, exiting the room.

"I am," Black said, winking at Kiss before leaving the room.

***

CHAPTER THIRTY-ONE

Black rode down the street silently, letting the wheels in his mind turn. He removed his phone and dialed Veronica Malone.

"This is Black, that plan we talked about. I will need you to expedite it. I overplayed my hand, and Berber's wife is about to be arrested, and I need you to get to her before they do."

"Why? Wouldn't it be better if we have her in custody, more leverage, right?"

"Wrong. We need Tamara to make the other parts work."

"Why are you so sure she'll do what you want her to?"

"She can't help herself; get her out. I'll handle the rest."

Black ended the call.

***

Trigger climbed from behind the driver's seat and closed the door, followed by Pepper Red, who got out on the passenger's side. It had been a mostly quiet ride, and neither spoke much. Trigger didn't feel awkward about the interaction; it was more of a reflective quietness. She agreed to ride with Pepper Red to meet with Big Heart, she had no idea what she was walking into, but she had given Pops her word that she would keep an eye on her, and she had no intention of breaking it.

They moved towards the lounge on 43rd, which didn't look like much on the outside. It was still early in the day, and they had yet to open for business.

"You know who owns this place?" Trigger asked as she opened the door and held it open for Pepper Red.

"It's been a while, but it was run by this guy we called the Old Jew. He wasn't Jewish, but it was a nickname that stuck. I doubt if he's still around."

After they both were inside, the door slowly closed behind them, leaving them in a dimly lit room. It smelled of sweat, fried food, and cigarette smoke, and it was one of the few places left in the city that ignored the no-smoking ordinance. A light-skinned woman with black hair down her back wearing a spaghetti strap blouse with the stomach out and hip-hugging jeans motioned for them to come to the bar.

She placed two napkins on the bar in front of the two women.

"You must be friends of Big Heart."

"We're here to meet him, but I certainly wouldn't call him a friend."

"What you drinking?"

"Cognac." Pepper Red said as she turned her back to the woman and scoped out the bar more now that her eyes had fully adjusted to the room's dimness.

The woman poured the drink, then looked to Trigger.

"And you?"

"A beer."

"Used to be a guy go by the name of Old Jew used to run this place; he still around?" Pepper Red asked as she turned and grabbed her glass from the bar.

"I'm Old Jew."

"The hell you are."

She smirked. "You mean my old man? I took over the place after he got on in age; the name kind of comes with the place."

"The old guy still around; that's good."

"Mind slips in and out; most days, he thinks it's still the old days. I used to bring him up here when he first retired; it helped him to be around the place. But as the years went by and more and more of his generation began dying off, moving away or just plain stopped coming, it seemed to make him more depressed not seeing any faces that he knew."

"Sorry to hear that. I always liked the guy."

"Yeah, should I tell him you said hi?"

"Nah, probably wouldn't remember me anyway; it's been a long time." It was a lie; Pepper Red was still a wanted woman. It made no sense to go throwing her name around, never knew who you were talking to.

"Where is Big Heart? I don't have all day."

Luther Allison's "Cherry Red Wine" came blaring through the speakers in the bar just as Big Heart entered from a room in the back of the bar, followed by Blake. Big Heart waved for Pepper Red to join him. She grabbed her glass of cognac and made her way to his table, followed by Trigger.

Pepper Red sat at the round table across from Big Heart. Blake sat at a table inches away from theirs and kept his eyes on Trigger. Trigger stood inches behind Pepper Red; she noticed the bandage on his hand; she ignored his weak attempts to look tough and kept her eyes trained on Big Heart.

Pepper Red downed her drink. "I'm here."

"Before we get into that, let's just take a moment."

"A moment for what?" Pepper Red asked as she reclined in her seat.

"A moment to take it all in; we've known each other a long time Pepper Red."

"And?"

"And we're still standing."

"Standing as opposition."

Big Heart laughed. "Shit, ain't it better to be alive as enemies than dead as allies? That ain't enough to reflect on life and be happy?"

"The fuck is this? You get locked up and come back, the Dalai Lama?"

"Not quite, inside, outside; one day, if you're lucky, you'll wake up and ask yourself if any of it was worth it?"

"Yeah, that's what you asked me here to see if I think any of it was worth it?"

Big Heart shook his head in defeat. "Not at all; that's a question only you can ask yourself. But I see you want to get to it so."

"Let's get to it."

"Right. My nephew gets killed."

"He does."

"You put down most of the bodies on the south side."

Pepper Red doesn't respond. He continues. "I get word that it was you, done in jealousy."

"Does that sound like something I would do?"

Big Heart shook his head no. "Not at first, but you are a woman."

"Women are weak-minded, love-struck, unstable emotional creatures, right?"

Big Heart threw his hands in the air. "As I said, you are a woman."

Pepper Red laughed. "I am."

"Before I can sit down with you, you flee the city; what am I supposed to think?"

"You're supposed to think I had the fucking FEDS on my head, and I was running for my life. You were supposed to think? Pepper Red loved Gerald; she wouldn't do that."

"Running for your life from the FEDS or me?"

"You answer that yourself, Big Heart. If I'm not scared to come to see you now, why in the hell would have I been scared to come to see you then? And you know, back then, I was a monster in these streets for me to touch you; it was nothing."

"That easy, huh?"

"Where do we go from here?"

Big Heart placed both hands on the table and ran his hands across the table calmly. "I sat locked up for almost two decades thinking about what I would do to you."

"So, it wasn't all peace, love, and reflection."

"I wanted to talk to you professional to professional to hear your side of it, and I figured I owed you that much. Now we let the cards land where they may."

"Look, I'm not running from a fight, never have, never will. I may get you; you may get me, you know what comes out of that?"

"An ending."

"Nope. Rather it's you, or if it's me in the end, all we get is one old dead gangster that no one remembers."

"I can't let it go, Pepper Red."

"I'm not asking you to, but don't you want to find out who did this?"

"And I'm supposed to do this how? Not many are still breathing from back then. Am I supposed to wait on that son of yours to figure it out?"

Pepper Red leaned in closer, resting her elbows on the table. Blake stood. Big Heart raised his hand calmly.

"Relax, it's not a threat, merely a question."

Blake took a step back, and looked up at Trigger; he noticed her eyes were locked on his. She was pushing her gun back into the holster. Pepper Red spoke as if she hadn't seen any interactions in the room. "Anything happens to him or Pope. I'm cutting down anyone I come across with your bloodline until I get to you."

"Again, what is your suggestion?"

"Give me a day or two."

"A truce?"

"For 48 hours, then you want to go to the mattresses, go to the mattresses."

"I might can do that, one stipulation."

"What's that?"

"You bring whoever did this to me before you put any holes in em."

Pepper Red shook her head no. "I'm not making any promises Big Heart."

"Yes, you are, or I hate to say it, but we've wasted our time this morning; nothing has changed."

"I'll do my best; that's all I can give you. May not be dead but won't promise they won't be bruised or bleeding."

"Now that that's out the way, don't you think we need to talk about the other thing?"

"I don't know where it is, Big Heart."

"Blake, why don't you and the pretty lady step out and let the grown folks talk for a little while."

Blake hesitated. Trigger didn't budge. Pepper Red looked at Trigger and nodded her approval.

"I'll be close by." Trigger said as she approached the exit with Blake following behind.

"You head on out too." Big Heart said loud enough for Old Jew to hear him. She came from behind the bar and made her way outside as well. Big Heart didn't speak again until the two were alone.

"Why in the hell did you come back, Pepper Red?"

"Heard you got out, wanted to see you."

Big Heart laughed. "Now, who's being sentimental."

"Not sentimental, practical."

"You want the bounty removed?"

"And my fucking name cleared."

"We all want something; I want my years back I gave to the penitentiary."

"Can't give you that one."

"But you can get me my money."

"I don't know where it is. I'm no fucking magician, and I'm as much in the dark about this as you are. I figured you and Gerald were in it together on the double cross, and I wrote that score off years ago. You should do the same." Pepper Red stood to leave.

"You do realize that there's no riding off into the sunset at the end of this one, don't you?"

She didn't respond. He spoke again. "You should've stayed gone, Pepper Red."

She paused, hand inside her jacket resting on the butt of her gun.

***

CHAPTER THIRTY-TWO

B lack sat behind the wheel of his car people watching. The men are dressed in colorful custom-made suits and alligator shoes, while the women wear everything from sequined minidresses to leather pantsuits. He watched Trigger step out of the lounge, joined by the young man he had shot in the hand at Big Heart's place and a woman that he'd never seen, no Pepper Red. He wondered if she had given Trigger the slip. Trigger didn't look worried, so he stayed in the car and continued watching.

He removed his phone, pulled up Google, and began doing his best search on Pepper Red. She was holding something back; all clients did, and she would be no exception. He pulled up a Public Records view, typed in her name, and found her Birth Certificate. He paid the fee and downloaded a copy to his phone.

He opened the file and read it, letting his eyes scan the particulars; it said she was born in Natchez, MS. Next, he looked up her high school. He remembered Pops told him they both went to Corliss.

He hoped they digitized old alum yearbooks, and they had. He keyed in the year she graduated and her name. Two students popped up with the last name Mohamed hers and a face he recognized, she was younger in the school photo, of course, but it was her. He downloaded both images and closed the app. He looked up just as he saw Pepper Red leave the lounge and approach their car. Trigger asked him to watch their backs; she didn't want Pepper Red to know. He watched as the couple chatting it up with Trigger got into a car sitting out front and pulled off. Pepper Red and Trigger also made it to their vehicle and drove off. He started the car and made a U-turn, heading in the opposite direction. He didn't need to follow them. Trigger would keep him in the loop about Pepper Red's movements.

***

Big Heart didn't pay much attention as someone else entered. Big Heart froze in his tracks when he saw who it was.

"Well, I'll be damned if it ain't officer Craig."

"That's detective, convict."

"A badge and a gun don't earn respect, boy; you got to stand on it with or without it.

"The pecking order has changed."

"Not from where I stand."

Craig pulled his gun and pointed it at Big Heart. "Hands on the bar, come on, let's go."

Big Heart did as he was told as Craig frisked him. He removed a switchblade and a revolver and placed both on the bar.

"Your parole office knows you have these?" Craig asked, laughing.

"Fuck you."

"Listen closely because I'm only asking once. Where's the score?"

"You think I would be in this shithole if I had it?"

"Someone knows where it is."

"My money is on Hambone."

"Berber don't know shit."

"Still his boy, I see."

"I'm nobody's boy." Big Heart laughed. Craig continued, "What about Pepper Red?"

"What about her?"

"Where is she?"

"Nigga, I just got out; how the hell am I supposed to know?"

"You better tell me something I want to hear real fucking soon."

"Or-" Before he could finish his sentence, Craig placed the gun to the back of his head and pulled the trigger.

***

CHAPTER THIRTY-THREE

B lack's phone vibrated as he drove, he looked at it sitting on his lap, and Stone's name flashed across the screen. He ignored it; he had yet to process it. He may be a father. He didn't know how he felt about that. He never thought past what they were doing even to consider having a family with her. They'd been messing around for a few years, and he barely knew her children. Then there was the issue with her ex popping up. She said he was gone, but would this be a regular occurrence of him popping in and out? Also, there was the issue of her living conditions. He understood that she did what she could as a single mother, but she would have to move if he were the baby's father; there was no way he was letting his child grow up like that. The phone stopped vibrating, and a few seconds later, the phone chimed. A voice message from Stone came th rough.

He ignored that alert as well. A few seconds later, his phone began chiming nonstop; back-to-back text messages flooded his phone for about thirty seconds. All from Stone, he ignored those as well, it was going to be uncomfortable, but it was time to put it all on the table and have a family reunion.

***

He had all the pieces on the table, but he wasn't sure if they all fit. In a not-so-straightforward way, it all started with him. Black pulled up to the house in Robertsdale, IN, thirty minutes outside Chicago. He turned the car off, checked his gun underneath his shirt, and got out. Black looked up at the house; it was modest-looking. Before going in, he looked around the neighborhood; he'd heard stories about Robertsdale but had never visited. He knew people from Chicago and Gary, IN, who had moved there for different reasons. Some to retire, some to hustle. Robertsdale was no Chicago or Gary, but if you took the streets for granted, something terrible could happen to you there just as quickly.

Black went up the stairs and knocked on the door; he waited a few seconds, and when no one answered, he knocked harder.

"Who is it?" A booming voice yelled through the door.

"Black, Black Love, I'm looking for Lion Mohamed."

Black heard the door unlock, and it swung open. Standing on the other side of the door was a yellow-hued black man towering over Black's five-foot frame. He was bulking and graying; he wore a black tank top and matching black sweatpants. He wore a black kufi on his head, and gray hairs covered his face in a long beard.

He looked Black up and down. "Come on in."

Black followed behind him as he led the way into his home. Black closed the door behind him and locked the door. The two men stood face to face. Lion hadn't offered him a seat, and he wouldn't ask.

"You know who I am?" Black asked, staring into his eyes with his hands in his pockets.

"I do."

"Aren't you surprised to see me?"

"Should I be?"

"Most grandfathers show emotion when they see their grandchildren."

"I'm not most grandfathers."

Black cleared his throat. The family reunion wasn't going how he expected, and the energy was off.

"I won't take too much of your time. I have some things we need to discuss."

"I'm listening."

"Pepper Red."

"Sharon."

"Yes, sir, Sharon."

"I didn't raise no damn Pepper Red; her name is Sharon Miner Mohamed."

"I hear you, Sharon."

"What about her?"

"What was her relationship with Tamara Mohamed?"

Lion smirked. "I'm not sure they had one."

"But you knew that they knew one another?"

"I did."

"Did they know that they were sisters?"

"If they did, neither said anything."

Black threw his hands in the air in disbelief. "You had these girls go to the same school and not tell them they were sisters?"

"I didn't want Tamara going there; her mother did it to be spiteful."

"And you take no responsibility for any of this?"

Lion stepped closer to Black. "You will not stand in my home and attempt to lecture me, get on with your questions."

Black took a step back. "That's it; I just wanted to hear it from your mouth. No more questions."

Black turned and walked back to the door.

"Tell your mother I said hello and to be safe."

Black paused with his back to the old man. He didn't respond; he opened the door and walked out.

***

CHAPTER THIRTY-FOUR

H e headed towards Stone's after the uncomfortable conversation with his grandfather and figured he might as well get all the uncomfortable discussions wrapped up in one night. He pulled in front of Stone's building and called her, and she answered on the first ring.

"Come open the door."

She ended the call without responding. Black placed his gun in the front of his pants and exited the car. He walked over to the security door and waited; not long after, she appeared and opened the door.

He had taken many a walk up these stairs, down this hall into her tiny two-bedroom apartment she shared with her four children. It usually ended with him lying in her bed, him having a drink, her smoking a blunt, and a sexual romp as a nightcap. He didn't have high hopes for tonight, going down a similar path.

Once inside, he was surprised to see the apartment was empty. Stone stopped at the kitchen table and sat. In all the years he's been coming over, he realized that he had never sat at the table, and they always went straight to the room. He followed her lead and sat.

"We need to talk Black."

"That's why I'm here."

"It's not cool ignoring my texts."

"It's not cool blowing my shit up like that. You know I'm working. What did you want anyway?"

"You didn't read the texts?"

"No."

She shook her head. "You are something else."

"So, what's up? What's on your mind?"

"What you think, Black?"

"Are you sure?"

"Nigga this ain't my first rodeo I know when I'm pregnant."

"Are you sure it's mine?"

"For the last time, my ex and I weren't like that, and he just stayed here for a little while, a one-time thing."

Black sighed.

"Don't get too excited nigga."

"Look, this my first time, alright. I went to the damn appointment with you. Shit, I just thought it would be different."

"Hmm, I did too. Shit, I thought I was done."

"What are you going to do?"

She laughed. "What do you mean what am I going to do?"

"You know?"

She stood and shook her head. "I know what?"

"Do you get a discount at work for situations like this?"

She laughed again. "You can't be serious, so since I work at Planned Parenthood, you think they give out discounts on abortions? Man, niggas will say anything."

"Oh, my God, Stone, don't make this a big fucking production."

"Negro please, if I were going get dramatic, you would know it. What you need to be doing is thinking of baby names because I don't believe in abortions."

"You're kidding, right?"

"Am I laughing?"

"You work at a damn abortion clinic and don't believe in abortions?"

"I'm pro-choice, they can do what they want with their bodies, and I do what I want with mine, hell I can earn a living; all drug dealers ain't dope fiends, right?"

"Great analogy, Stone."

"Fuck you, Black; think what you want as long as you don't miss the point."

"I get it."

"You get what?"

"I get it, Stone; just give me time to process it. I thought I would be married first."

"Well, before you drop to one knee, I ain't marrying you."

Black laughed. "Good cause I ain't asking."

She walked over and sat on his lap. "Aren't you just a little bit happy about it?"

Black forced a smile. "Yeah, I am low-key."

She pressed his forehead with her finger pushing his head back. "You are such a fucking liar. It's alright; give it some time; you will be happy, trust me." She leaned in and kissed Black on his lips.

"I'm sure I will be." As the words left his mouth, he didn't know if he meant that or was trying to spare her feelings.

***

CHAPTER THIRTY-FIVE

B lack woke up the following day to banging at his door. Wrestling himself from the comfort of his sheets, he went to the door. Black opened the door, and he was surprised and upset when he saw who it was; typically, he would tell Bosselait to kick rocks showing up at his home unexpectedly and uninvited. When they'd known one another, he had never shown up at his house before, and Black didn't like it, but with everything going on with Pepper Red, he needed to know what he knew and see if it connected.

"Can I come in?" Bosselait asked in what Black assumed was the most professional tone he could come up with.

"Why not? It must be important you come to my home; where's your partner?"

"She had shit to do."

Black turned and led the way back into his living room; he pointed at the couch and went to the kitchen.

"I'm about to put a pot on; you want a cup?"

"I'll pass."

He ignored the gesture for the offer to sit and followed Black into the kitchen; looking around the room, he stationed himself at the kitchen entrance.

"What can I do for you, Bosselait?"

"William Mossberry."

"Big Heart, what about him?"

"He's dead."

Black was shocked by the news. Pepper Red had just seen Big Heart the day before. He was sure Big Heart was alive and kicking when she and Trigger left yesterday, but there was no way for him to know. Trigger and the young boy had both stepped outside, and she could have done it then. He had his back to the detective, and he remained silent. Bosselait continued.

"We found a phone on him."

Black turned and faced Bosselait as he waited for the coffee to brew. "Yeah."

"Yeah, we traced it back to a Satchel Chatman, a.k.a. Scat-Man I know that name rings a bell."

Black didn't respond. He turned, grabbed a coffee mug from the cabinet, and poured himself a cup. Bosselait continued.

"We traced Satchel's previous calls that led us to-"

"My doorstep."

Bosselait chuckled. "Fucking grade, A detective here."

"What do you want, Bosselait?"

"I want to know what you and Scat-Man were talking about."

"Nothing really; he was looking to hire me for some work, possibly."

Bosselait rolled his eyes. "Work, huh? What did he want you to investigate?"

"Don't know, never got passed what my rates were, said he would think about it, never heard back from him."

"Never heard back, huh?"

Black clutched his cup with both hands. "That's what I said."

"How are you with math Black?"

"Fuck the riddles, Bosselait, spit it out."

"Stay here with me, math...by my count, that's three." He held up three fingers in the air for dramatic effect. Black didn't miss the implication and stared back, not speaking. Bosselait continued. "Three dead men since your mother's been back in town. Rucker, Big Heart, and Scat-Man."

"Three dead men since my mother has allegedly been back in town."

Bosselait smiled. "Fucking lawyers. She allegedly killed these men." Bosselait said, holding up two fingers on both hands using air quotes.

"It's time for you to go," Black said, placing his cup on the counter.

"She has to come in Black, and it'll go a hell of a lot smoother if she does."

"I don't know how else to say it. I haven't seen her, and as far as the bodies dropping, people die daily in Chicago; I'm pretty sure my mother had nothing to do with those deaths either." Black followed behind Bosselait as he headed back towards the door. "And detective, don't show up at my door again uninvited."

Standing on the other side of the door in the hall, Bosselait turned and faced Black. "You don't want to be on the wrong side of this thing, counselor."

"Wrong side, right side doesn't matter. I'm on the side with my mother." Black said, closing the door before Bosselait could respond.

***

CHAPTER THIRTY-SIX

Black played it smooth with Bosselait there, but on the inside, he was panicking. He knew there was a good chance that he was right. It looked as if someone was cleaning up, and all the people involved in the robbery from 97 were being wiped off the board individually. He retrieved the burner phone Pepper Red had given him and dialed her number. He placed it on speaker, set it on his dresser, and scrambled to get dressed as it rang. It rang until it got to voicemail. He ended the call without leaving a message. He picked up his other phone and dialed Trigger, and she picked it up after the third ring.

"Trigger."

"What's up?"

"She with you?"

"Nah."

"Cool, talk later?"

"Yeah."

He ended the call and dialed Pops. "What's good old man?"

"Nothing much; how are you, son?"

"Chilling was going stop by. Can I bring you anything?"

"I'm fine. I don't need anything."

"You hear anything about Trigger's new friend?"

"I hadn't heard anything."

"Cool, see you in a few."

Black ended the call. He cursed under his breath. They were speaking in code. It wasn't the most complex code, but he got the point. He hadn't heard from

Pepper Red, and he had no idea where to begin to look for her. For all he knew, she could be out of town again.

After getting dressed, he sat on the edge of his bed and breathed. He was jumping to conclusions. If Bosselait was trying to rattle his cage, he was doing a good job, he thought. He took another deep breath. He relaxed. He told himself he called once; she could still be asleep. He would wait until she returned the call. Maybe she had answers as to why everyone from the heist was suddenly coming up dead. Even if she would admit to the heist, she wasn't the most forthcoming.

Black made his way to his desk in his office. He pulled out his chair and sat behind his desk. Opening his desk drawer, Black removed the photo of his mother and the other suspects from the robbery. He pulled a red sharpie and began placing a red X across the face of each dead member. Three remained: Pepper Red, Craig, and the unidentified person's arm with the figure eight tattoo, which he guessed was Berber's wife, Tamara.

Things were starting to become more apparent now. No one had tried to kill his mother yet. At least not as far as he knew, but the way things were looking, not only did this unidentified killer want the members from the heist dead, but Pepper Red still had the bounty on her head and the police after her. There was a good chance one of the three remaining members was the killer, Pepper Red included.

Staring at the photo, he paused. The bounty, Big Heart, was killed before he could lift the bounty on his mother's head. He redialed her and, as before, got only the voicemail.

He stood from his desk and figured he would head to the office to check what the kids were up to. He looked around his home office. He would have to clear it out and put some things in storage. Johnny couldn't keep sleeping at the office, and he needed a better sense of stability and supervision. He would take some of Mickey's money and get him a bed for the room. His phone rang, and the name across the screen read Veronica; he answered on the first ring.

"What's up?"

"We have a problem."

"What kind of problem?"

"She got away?"

Black kept walking; now, in the hall, he continued towards the elevator to get to his underground garage.

"How? I thought you had people on her?"

"I did; she gave them the slip."

"We need her to make this work."

"That's why I'm calling. I took a big risk getting Tamara out of the facility. Berber will not take this lightly, and he holds a lot of weight in this town. Do you know where she might be headed or who she might call?"

"When I spoke with her, she made it seem like she had no one, but I know where she's probably going. I'll text you the address and meet you there."

Black ended the call.

***

CHAPTER THIRTY-SEVEN

N ow in his car, Black was headed to see Berber; halfway there, the burner phone rang; it was Pepper Red; he told her to meet him in an hour, gave her the address, and ended the call. He dialed Veronica back; she picked up on the first ring.

"I need you to do something for me."

"Don't you always Black? What is it?"

"Get me an off-the-books meeting with Berber."

"What do you mean by off the books? What are you talking about, an ambush?"

"Don't act like it's beneath you. I remember being thrown at your feet in one of those meetings just days ago."

"Look, I apologize for that, it was a bit much, and I did talk with my guys about it, but look, this guy is an Alderman."

"I'm not as important. I get it."

"That's not what I'm saying."

"Look, I'm not bothered by what occurred. Can you do the meet or not?"

Veronica went silent for a few beats before responding. "When?"

"Within the hour."

"I'll text you the time and place." She ended the call.

***

Twenty minutes later, Black was pulling up behind Luella's on E. 53rd. He parked, got out, and banged on the backdoor. A few seconds later, someone wearing a baseball cap, checkered pants, a chef's jacket, and an apron opened the door. He was ushered inside and led to the kitchen. Standing in the kitchen was Veronica, a few employees, and Berber. Black nodded at the group, and Berber had his head over a pot of turnip greens taking in the aroma. When he raised his head and turned back to Veronica, he was surprised to see Black.

"Can we have the room for a few minutes, guys?" Veronica asked, directed towards the employees. They all promptly left the room leaving the three alone.

"What is this, Veronica? You ask me here under the guise of going in with the owner and opening franchises through the Midwest only to be blitz-attacked?"

Veronica held up her hands in a non-defensive manner.

"Did I have a sleight of hand when getting you to meet me here? Yes, but no one's here to attack you."

"Sleight of hand, my dick, what is that lawyer talk for lie?"

"I needed to talk to you alone and without being seen." Black said, interjecting himself into the conversation."

"And with that, I am out of here. The owner did this for me as a favor, so you two be civil and clear out in ten minutes. They're opening for business soon." Veronica said as she went back out of the restaurant through the back door.

"What do you want, Love?"

"Oh, so you do know who I am?"

"Cut the shit; the fact that you asked for this meet-up, Veronica told you about the favor I asked of her, and she's chosen whose side she's on."

"No sides to be chosen, Alderman. I'm here to do a favor for you."

"And that is?"

"I'm here to save your life."

"I don't have time for this." Berber walked towards the door. Black blocked his path and removed the photo of the bank robbers from his jacket pocket, handing it to Berber. Berber looked at the picture. "What is this?"

"You know what it is."

"Let's pretend I don't."

"It's the crew from the First National Bank heist of 97. You know, the one where the money was never recovered."

"And this has something to do with me. How?"

"I was trying to figure out why the hit was placed on my mother for G-Man's murder. Her killing him was one thing, but it didn't make sense for her to be marked for death for decades over a crime of passion. Then I found out about the missing money. Now twenty million dollars will always be a driving force for revenge no matter how many years it's been."

"I am in no way implicating myself in any crimes. I do not know about a bank robbery, a murder, or an alleged death bounty being placed on your mother, the wanted fugitive of the United States government Sharon Miner Mohamed's head. Furthermore, I have no idea why you think any of this has anything to do with me."

"So, you don't notice the red X marks on all the faces in the picture?"

"I do."

"And in case you aren't catching on, the red X's are over the faces of the newly deceased."

Berber looked at his watch. "Are we going somewhere with this?"

"True, you aren't in this picture, but the way I figure this is the crew, but not all the crew. At first, I thought Big Heart might have been the bankroll financing the heist, but the one taking the picture is probably the financier. If I had to put my money on it, the photographer is probably you, Alderman Hambone."

Berber smirked. Black continued. "Do yourself a favor and tell me who wants your old crew dead, unless that's not you that took the picture. Think twice before answering Alderman because the killer is on a streak right now."

"Hypothetically speaking."

"Of course."

"I would put my money on Pepper Red."

"Bullshit."

"Bodies didn't start dropping until she got back in town."

"Until she allegedly got back in town."

"Allegedly my ass, if not her, then who? It sure the hell ain't me."

"If, and I mean a mighty big if, it's not you that leaves Craig, my mother, or Tamara."

Berber laughed. "Tamara, who, my wife?"

"I know she was a part of the crew Berber."

"Now you want to implicate my wife in these bogus charges; who's next, huh? My mom, maybe?"

Black laughed. "Why not? You accused my mother; how do I know that's not your mother holding the camera taking the picture?"

"Get to what you want, or I'm out of here."

"A pardon for my mother."

"In exchange for what?"

"A confession from the killer."

"You're insane, and they're just going to confess openly? I don't have that kind of authority anyway."

"Call in some favors unless you don't think your life is worth it. And to answer your question, you're damn right they won't be able to help themselves."

"Don't con me, Love."

"No con, just give me your word; you'll make the calls to make the pardon happen."

"If it is what you say it is, you have my word."

***

CHAPTER THIRTY-EIGHT

After meeting with Black, Berber was having a drink in his office behind his desk. Not long after, a tap on the door was nudged open, and Craig stepped in and nodded at Berber.

"Where is everyone? It's like a ghost town out there."

"I sent everyone home."

"What was so urgent?"

"Take a load off, have a drink."

"It's not a social call, Berber; what's up?"

"Needed to know how things were coming along in the streets?"

"I'm making progress."

"She ain't in custody yet."

Berber laughed. "Custody, aye, is that what we're calling it now?"

"Love came to see me."

"No shit, what he say?"

"He knows about the job in 97."

"You don't say."

"You're not surprised."

"You are? Pepper Red must have told him."

Berber swallowed what was left of the liquor in his glass, poured another shot, and shook his head no. "He's sticking to the he hasn't seen her story."

"And you believe him?"

Berber shrugged his shoulders and took another swallow of his drink. Craig spoke again.

"What else he say?"

"He found the money."

Craig laughed. "Bullshit."

Berber didn't respond verbally; he raised an eyebrow and leaned back into his seat. Craig spoke again.

"He tell you where it was?"

"He did."

"Why would he do that?"

"Wants a pardon for his mother."

"The mother he claims to have not seen; you aren't buying this, are you?"

"That's why I'm pulling you in on it; it could be a trap."

"A trap?"

"Yeah, he's said something about the crew that pulled the job coming up dead one after the other. You know anything about that?"

Craig stepped closer to the desk. "Where did he say the money was?"

"Said something about Lil G Man having a property in Fernwood."

"I guess he did figure it out; you speak to any of your judges on the payroll about the pardon?"

Berber shook his head no.

"What do you mean he figured it out?"

"Yeah, I don't know how, but she got out."

'Who?"

"Tamara, she brought me in on it; we killed Lil G Man all those years ago. We were supposed to get the money and run away together; you never appreciated her."

"What are you, a bond villain? Why are you telling me all of this?"

Craig laughed. "The thing is, I killed Lil G Man before he told her where the money was; overzealous, I guess."

Berber shook his head. "You are a special kind of stupid, aren't you?"

"I outsmarted you, and to answer your question, it doesn't matter that I'm telling you all of this; you won't be around to repeat it."

Craig pulled his gun and shot Berber twice in the chest; he watched for a few seconds as the blood oozed and Berber stopped moving. He turned and then left the room.

***

CHAPTER THIRTY-NINE

The sun had gone down as Craig approached the property in Fernwood, IL. He drove around to the back, parked, got out of his car, opened the trunk, and removed a shovel, a generator, and a generator-powered tower light. Craig reached a patch of grass near the property and turned on the light. As he picked up the shovel, a figure emerged from the shadows.

"It took you long enough."

"Save the jokes, Tamara, rest up. I ain't digging this hole alone."

"I'll carry my weight; just start digging."

The two dug into the earth until six feet into the ground.

"I found something," Craig yelled as he struggled to get one of the three bags over his head. "Get over here and help me."

Tamara helped to pull the bags out of the ground until all three were out. Once Craig was out of the hole, they both held their breath as Craig unzipped the bag and they peered into it. They both sighed as they laughed, staring into the bag at the stacks of hundred-dollar bills. They hugged and kissed before Tamara reached into the bag and grabbed a stack. Her face morphed into a frown as she felt her fingertips become wet.

"What the hell is this?"

A look of concern crossed Craig's face as he reached into the bag and grabbed a stack. "What's wrong?"

"No." She dropped the stack and grabbed another bundle of hundreds. "No, no, no!"

"What's wrong, guys?"

Startled, they both turned around to find Black, Veronica, Bunchy, Berber, and Bosselait all standing behind them.

"What the hell is this?" Craig asked, annoyed.

"Guess you didn't know. After a while, the ink begins to run on US currency, huh? Yeah, I had a buddy who was into some bad things years ago, buried some money in his mom's backyard, did six years came home, dug it up, and it was just like yours." Black said as he laughed.

"You were in on this, Berber?" Craig asked, disappointed.

Berber wearing a bulletproof vest, tossed an empty plastic blood pack at Craig's feet.

"It took some convincing on Love's part; shit, there was no guarantee you wouldn't shoot me in the head. But he was right."

"I should've taken a headshot."

Berber laughed. "Not about that, about you confessing the whole thing."

"Yeah, I told you, Berber, I have this way of reading people, and I knew he couldn't help himself without ever meeting him. In almost every story I heard about you two, he was always in your shadow. It made him resentful. He always needed you, so he pushed his hate for you deep down inside. When he thought he didn't need you anymore, it was too much for him not to rub it in your face how Craig thought he was better and smarter than you."

Berber laughed. "Smarter than me?"

Craig reached for his gun. He paused when he saw swarms of red beams covering him and Tamara.

"Yeah, if you haven't figured it out, we got you covered."

Craig took his hand off his gun and put his hands in the air.

"So, you used me," Tamara said, speaking for the first time since they arrived.

"Your greed made it easy," Black said, stepping aside to allow Bunchy to handcuff her.

"I bet that mental facility looks nice right about now?" Craig said as he laughed.

"Wait a minute; I'll make a deal; he was in on it, I'll testify," Tamara said as she got led out of the yard.

"You can try, but nothing is connecting me to the heist, and Craig, in case you're wondering, yes, I did record the conversation in my office, video, and audio."

"You son of a bitch!" Craig yelled, being dragged out by two officers.

Bosselait spoke for the first time. "Where's your mother?"

"I don't know. I sent the address."

"Did you tell her about the deal?"

"Nah, she wouldn't have shown up."

"I'll have my office put in the paperwork; Berber's judge reached out to me about it; you talk to her and let her know she's no longer a wanted woman," Veronica said as she nodded at the men before leaving the yard. Berber nodded at Black and went as well. Black was behind him, and Bosselait grabbed him by the arm.

"A word."

Black turned a faced him. "What's up?"

"Ever heard of a Tin-Tin Gravanni?"

Black crossed his arms across his chest. "Should I have?"

"You never know; he's a snitch of mine doing five to nine in Joliet."

"What about him?"

"Told me to get word to you that the bounty on Pepper Red has been lifted."

"Who is this Tin-Tin, he connected?"

"Small time, not even associate ties."

"Then how is what he says credible?"

"He has a reputation for information and getting the word out about things inside and out here. If he says the bounty is lifted, it's lifted."

"I understood that only Big Heart can have it removed, and he was dead before he could."

"Someone in high places has a soft spot for Pepper Red."

"Thanks for the message Bosselait."

Bosselait nodded and left the yard. Black looked around the yard at the piles of dirt, the hole, the tower light, and crime scene investigators as they secured the perimeter. He removed his burner phone and dialed Pepper Red. The phone rang once, and this line has been disconnected message came on. Black smirked, tossed the phone into the hole, and left the yard.

***

"What now?" Noble asked Pepper Red as he dumped the ashes from his blunt out the window of the car they were sitting in.

"Back to Detroit."

"You don't want to follow him? Wait until he's alone; tell him."

"Nah, he's not ready; let's go home."

Pepper Red watched as Black walked back to his car; they made a U-Turn and went in the opposite direction.

***

Walking back to his car, Black looked at his phone, and there were a handful of missed calls from Stone. He placed the phone back on his hip, got in his car, and hit the highway. Twenty minutes later, he was sitting in Wicker Park. The neighborhood of Brownstones lining the block was quiet and serene. It was just before sunrise. He got out of his car, checked his gun, and placed it in the front of his pants, covering it with his shirt. He walked up to the address he was looking for, went up the stairs, and knocked on the door. It wasn't long after the door opened.

"What's going on, Deborah?"

Deborah Kiss staring back, red hair tied into a bun, wearing a sheer white gown, grabbed Black by the shirt and pulled him into the house.

The End

SNEAK PEEK: THE 13TH PROSPECT STRANDED ON STONY ISLAND A BLACK LOVE DETECTIVE STORY BOOK 6

CHAPTER ONE

"How did we get here?" The towering figure asked as he stood face to face with the frightened woman. She stared wide-eyed as he wrapped his hands around her neck and squeezed. She clawed at his arms to get free with no luck. He pressed her forcefully against the wall. Staring into her eyes he repeated. "How did we get here." A smirk creased his face as he felt the fight fade, and he began getting an erection. "Why are you doing this to me?" he asked in an airy breath. Her legs began giving way as she slouched against the wall, no fight left as he allowed her to fall to the floor, him falling with her still squeezing. His eyes bulged from his face, saliva pooling in his mouth, running down his chin as he felt the last of life slip from her and he ejaculated in his pants.

Panting and out of breath he stood and peered down at her. "I expected more of a fight."

"What now boss?" A voice from behind him asked.

"Search the place see if you can find anything that'll point me to my money."

***

Amanda Moore's frantic race against the clock was a symphony of anxiety. Chain-smoking three Newport's and a quick sip of wine, her nerves finally found their footing. In the mirror, she assessed herself with surgical precision, every detail falling into place. Satisfied, she gave her apartment a lightning-quick once-over and hustled toward the door. Her keys beckoned by the entrance, but she hesitated, flinging open the closet to snatch a silk scarf to hide the damning bruises.

Then, a sudden sound cracked the air, her heart beating like a drum. A man's thundering footsteps erupted from the closet. Action snapped her into a frenzy. With trembling hands, she shifted the lifeless body with a dancer's grace, avoiding the spreading bloodstain. Her fingers closed around the scarf, her gaze lingering on the deceased man, a knife piercing his chest. In a breathless prayer, she sealed the closet door, concealing the gruesome secret.

In over her head, she thought she had the upper hand on Sheek, but reality hit hard. She'd moved, believing she'd evaded detection until she sorted things out. Now, with her daughter's phone silent and a corpse in her closet, her options dwindled. She pushed away fears for her daughter. They'd talked last night, and she'd promised to flee to Milwaukee to stay with a friend. She was sure she'd escaped Chicago, or at least that was the hope she clung to. Until her daughter called, wishful thinking was her lifeline.

"Hold the door!" A man called out, with a slight African accent, she didn't know which country he was from, it wouldn't had mattered it annoyed her all the same. She let the security door slam closed. She hustled toward her car. The man looked on holding a box in his arms, annoyed, shaking his head. "Damn foreigners," she muttered, her mind racing.

***

ABOUT THE AUTHOR

Antwan Floyd Sr. is an American novelist, most widely recognized for his crime fiction. He has written a series of best-selling mysteries featuring the hard-boiled detective Black Love, a black private investigator living in Chicago, IL; they are perhaps his most popular works.

www.ingramcontent.com/pod-product-compliance
Lightning Source LLC
Chambersburg PA
CBHW050409030726
47503CB00006B/2106